God's Shield

By

Ronna M. Bacon

ISBN 978-1-998821-37-2

Psalm 91:4. He shall cover you with His feathers, and under His wings you shall take refuge; His truth shall be your shield and buckler.

Proverbs 30:5. Every word of God is pure; He is a shield to those who put their trust in Him.

NKJV

Table of Contents

Chapter 1

With his hand reaching for the fragile, small branches of a nearby tree, Teeg Callahan carefully balanced himself on the wet log that he had stepped onto. His foot slipped for a moment before he regained his balance and carefully crept along the only way across the creek. The creek was tumbling in a wild manner just below the fallen tree trunk, splashing across it and making Teeg's path even more hazardous. He stared down at his feet as he paused for a moment, a hand still reaching to grasp at a sturdier branch. He was only halfway across the log and he felt that he just could not make it. His border collie, Andy, waited for him, barking once in a while for Teeg to hurry up.

Finally, his foot reached for solid ground. He paused to catch his breath. He dropped to his knees, a hand on the ground bracing himself. His hand went back up to help slide the body that was draped across his shoulder carefully to the ground. The body hit limply in front of him and did not move.

This was not what he had planned on for that day. He was out with his dog, trying to assess the wildlife at the creek for his work as a wildlife biologist when he had noticed a pile of clothing on the other side of the creek. Teeg had frowned before he had made his way across the log and knelt. Teeg was shocked as he brushed aside golden blonde curls to see the white, pain-filled face of a beautiful lady. He looked around, not sure why she was there. They were out in the wild, miles from town. He frowned at the camera bag that lay beside her.

Teeg had drawn the lady to her feet and then carefully draped her over his shoulder. He had no other option in order to get her to the other side of the creek. The camera bag was shoved over his shoulder before his arm was around her jean-clad legs and he started the dangerous path to the other side. Andy barked at him as he began his trek.

Staring down at her face, Teeg worried about the lady. He was a couple of miles away from his cabin and that meant he had to carry her. He watched as Andy crept closer and laid his head on the lady's leg. He looked around, searching for just what he didn't know. He looked up at the clear blue summer sky, his thoughts troubled.

Reaching for the camera bag, he draped it across his body. He sighed to himself, knowing that he had to move. He began to pray, begging God to awaken the lady. He didn't know what to do and only God could direct his steps. He was confident in that. God had provided and guided him throughout his life. This was no different. The only thing different was that he was in an unusual situation of having a lady to look after. He had no idea how to do that.

Teeg gathered the lady into his arms, her head settling against his shoulder. He stared down at her, a frown on his face. He thought that he knew her but he had no idea where from. He began to walk carefully over the rough ground, heading for his cabin. It would take time, he knew, hearing the sounds of nature around him. Andy paced at his side, his head tilting up to watch the lady. He understood, it seemed, that even though she was a stranger, Teeg would look after her. Andy was used to being out and about with Teeg during the day.

Reaching his rough-looking log cabin, Teeg carefully set the lady into one of the chairs on the front deck and reached for his keys. The door was unlocked quickly and Teeg was inside, pulling the camera bag over his head and then dropping it onto a table near the door. He looked behind him and through the door, watching the lady for a moment, before he turned. He rubbed at his cheek, not sure what he was to do. Teeg headed for the single bedroom, pulling back the covers. He had changed the bed that morning, not his usual day of doing so but God had nudged him to do that. He had learned early in life to follow God's nudges.

Returning to the front door, Teeg hesitated. He had no idea who the lady was and he would need to determine that. First, though, he had to get her inside and then assess what he needed to do for her. Not that he would be able to do much. He was not a medical person, only having the rudimentary training.

Gathering the lady into his arms once more, Teeg stared down at her. His light brown eyes held concern and worry about her. The light breeze tossed the dark brown hair around his head, frustrating him. He then stalked towards the bedroom, deposited the lady before he pulled off her hiking boots, setting them to one side, and then tucking the blankets around her. He then headed for the living room and reached for her camera bag. He hesitated, asking God for permission to snoop.

He didn't like to do that but in this case, he had no choice.

Andy licked at Teeg's hand before he paced into the bedroom. His head turned as he listened to Teeg's quiet movements and then turned back to the bed. A single leap and he was on the bed, snuggled tight to the lady.

Teeg gently opened the camera bag, setting out the equipment. It was not cheap, he could tell, and professional in nature. He frowned as he turned his head to stare towards the bedroom. His fingers found a business card and pulled it out. Triese Cameron? He didn't know her. Now, why was she out there?

Carefully packing away the equipment in as much of the order as he could remember, Teeg walked to the bedroom door to stare at Triese. Her eyes had flickered open briefly as he had laid her down, showing deep blue eyes of a shade that he had never seen before. He didn't understand what had happened to her or why she was out there. God did but He wasn't sharing that with him at the moment.

A sound outside drew his attention and he paced towards the door, a hand reaching for the door handle. The door flew open and slammed back against the wall. Teeg's hands were in the air as he backed away from the two men who charged into his home. A hand dropped as he grabbed for Andy's collar, keeping the dog from flying at the man. Andy's bark sounded loud in the air, the anger in the bark and growl obvious to everyone that Andy was angry and ready to attack.

Forced away from the door and then into a chair, Teeg frowned. He didn't know the men or why they were there. One man stood in front of him, his arms crossed over his chest. The other man explored the cabin. Teeg watched him disappear into the bedroom before he was back out and beckoning the first man towards him. Their conversation was low enough that Teeg could not understand the words. He watched their faces darken in anger before the second man paced out of the cabin. The first man planted himself in front of the door and kept a watch on Teeg.

Andy slinked away from Teeg, heading for Triese. He was on the bed, facing the door, his nose on his paws. He was alert to any danger that would approach the lady who his master had rescued. He would do everything that he could to protect her for Teeg.

Teeg kept his eyes on the man. He didn't know either one and had no idea what they wanted. They seemed to be interested in Triese and that worried him. He had no idea why.

Hours passed with Teeg kept in his chair. The second man had appeared at the door, speaking quietly to the first man before he disappeared again. Teeg watched them, trying to puzzle out what was happening. All he could understand was that God was in control and that He would protect both himself and Triese. Teeg just didn't know what from.

Chapter 2

Early evening found Teeg still seated in his chair. He could hear Andy moving restlessly before the dog found him. Teeg frowned down at the dog and then at the door. The man who had been stationed inside had cracked open the door a couple of hours previously and then disappeared. Teeg had been too shaken to move, not certain if the man would return.

On his feet, Teeg paced quietly towards the door. His hand rested on it for a moment before he opened the door cautiously and let Andy out. He stepped outside and watched as Andy ran around the yards and around the house before he came back to Teeg's side and nudged at his hand.

Teeg stared down at Andy before he made his own inspection of his home and yard. The men had disappeared. Neither one had said anything at all, just stared at him. Teeg had not questioned them, almost afraid to find out what they wanted.

Turning back into his house, he reached for food to fill Andy's bowl and then refreshed his water. He turned for a moment, staring back at the door before shaking his head. He had no idea who the men were or what they wanted. He had not recognized them and neither man had spoken. He praised God that Triese and he had not been harmed. Teeg was still puzzled by why Triese had been out there. He shrugged as he reached to prepare his supper before he walked to the bedroom doorway. He could not eat until he had spoken with her.

Teeg paced towards the bed, seeing that Triese had not moved. He frowned, trying to think of how to pronounce her name. It was very unusual, just as his was. He returned to the kitchen to grab a bottle of water. Uncapping it, Teeg lifted Triese enough so that she could sip at the bottle. A softly-spoken thanks caused him to pause as he was laying her back down. He was frustrated, he knew. He wanted answers and those not were forthcoming.

Late that evening, Teeg paced his cabin. He had retrieved a pillow and blanket from his linen closet and dropped them on his couch. It was not the first time that he had slept there. This was different though. He was on edge and didn't know why. Andy had not been alerting to anyone around his cabin and Teeg knew full well that he would if someone had been outside.

His attention turned to the bedroom doorway and he paused his steps. He had been in and out, checking up on Triese. By tomorrow, he knew that he would need to head into town with her. He just didn't want to leave his home. Teeg had been very stressed lately and found that his cabin was the only place where he felt safe and at peace. His work drew him there as well. Monitoring the animals in the area had been his work for years now and he had no desire to move anywhere else.

Finally seeking his rest, Teeg prayed for the lady who had so suddenly appeared in his life. He wanted to know who she was and where she had come from. Those answers would come at some point. It didn't help that he wanted them right then.

Early in the morning, Triese's eyes cracked open just a bit. She moved restlessly in the bed, shifting to her side and pulling the blankets up on her neck. She yawned, not sure what was going on. It didn't feel like her own bed. Jumping as she heard a rustling near her, Triese froze before she felt a wet tongue swipe at her face. A dog? She didn't have a dog. That she was certain of. She sighed, an arm out to wrap around the dog before she slept. Andy snuggled closer to the lady who his master had rescued. She was now part of his family, he decided, and he would do his best to protect her.

After a restless night of broken sleep, Teeg was on his feet. He searched for Andy before he stopped just outside of the bedroom. A small smile crossed his face. Andy was content to be held by Triese, his eyes turning towards his master. Teeg could see Andy's reluctance to leave the lady he was protecting when he called him. He grinned again as the dog finally jumped from the bed and ran for the door. Teeg knew that Andy would be back in and beside Triese just as soon as he could.

His mug of coffee in his hand, Teeg stepped outside, drawing in a deep breath of the freshness of the early morning. He could hear the sounds of nature around him. This was Teeg's favourite time of the day. It reminded him of the freshness of God's love that was renewed each day. He usually felt peace at this time of day. Today, he didn't. He was too worried about Triese and the danger that seemed to be encompassing her.

Andy returned to stand up at Teeg, reaching to lick at his master's face as he bent down to rub at Andy's ears. Teeg then walked around the cabin, searching for anything that was out of the ordinary, sipping at his coffee as he did so. Hearing a door opening at the front of the cabin, Andy ran that way, a happy yip coming from him. Teeg followed somewhat slower, standing for a moment to stare at Triese. He frowned before he moved forward, his voice quiet as he told Andy to sit.

Triese jumped, scared as she hear a man's voice. She had no idea where she was or who the man was in front of her. Her eyes were huge as she stared at him.

"Who are you? And just where am I?" Triese spun in a circle, reaching out a hand to find something to balance herself against. She was off balance and dizzy and didn't like that feeling. She prayed for safety, not knowing who the man was standing in front of her with a smile on his face.

"I'm Teeg Callahan. I found you on the other side of the creek yesterday. You were unconscious. I have no idea what happened to you." He pointed to a chair. "Sit. Do you drink coffee?" At her nod, he lifted his mug. "I'll go find you some. Cream and sugar?" Again she nodded, watching as Teeg disappeared into the house. He returned in short order and handed her the mug of coffee. He sat nearby, a hand resting on Andy's head.

Triese sipped at her coffee, her eyes searching the area around her. She was terrified but she had no idea why.

“Can I ask how you pronounce your name? I apologize. I looked through your camera case to find out who you are.” Teeg was contrite at that. He felt as if he had invaded her privacy.

“It’s “Trace”. I am named after an Irish great-grandmother.” She shifted to stare at him. “I need to know your name.”

“It’s Teeg Callahan. I live here. I work as a wildlife biologist.” Teeg sipped at his own coffee, not sure what more to say. He was concerned about Triese without knowing why.

“I see. I’m a wildlife photographer. I’ve traveled the world and have never been in such a situation as this. Where are we?” Triese looked around, not afraid of Teeg but afraid of why she couldn’t remember that she was in danger. That she was in danger, she had no doubt.

Teeg watched her, a hand resting on Andy’s head. He needed to question her further but he didn’t feel comfortable doing that. This was not how his day was to go. It was Saturday and he needed to head into the small town of Red Oak to buy his weekly supplies.

Chapter 3

Triese was uneasy. She clutched her mug, staring around where she could see. She was out in the wilderness, she decided, with someone she didn't know. Or did she? Triese turned to face Teeg, finding him with his head bowed and his eyes closed. Either he was asleep or praying. She couldn't decide which one.

"How far are we from town?" Triese winced at the raspiness of her voice.

Teeg raised his head, his eyes on the horizon. He nodded before he turned to face her himself.

"About five miles from the road. To the road? It's about a mile following the trail. My truck is parked about halfway there in the garage that had built there. I'll get you to town, Triese. Is that where you live?"

Triese drew in a deep breath. Whispering a prayer that she could trust him, she nodded.

"I do. I have for about five years. I made it my base." She bit at her lip. "I'm taking you away from your tasks for the day."

"Not a problem, Triese. You need me. Where's your car?" Teeg had tried to puzzle that out.

"My car? I don't remember. I know that I was at home yesterday morning and had no interest in going anywhere. I was working on some photos for a client. Then this morning, I'm here. Who did this? And why?"

"I can't help with that. Not yet, Triese. But I will try my best to help you solve it. I also have a brother on the local police force. He'll work with you as well." Teeg was on his feet, reaching for her mug. "Stay here. I'll be back with some breakfast for us."

Teeg was as good as his work, handing her a plate of pancakes and bacon before he was into the cabin again and returning with fresh mugs of coffee. His head was down as he asked a blessing over their meal. They ate with minimal conversation.

Reaching for her plate, he stacked it with his. He studied her, seeing the dark shadows under her beautiful eyes. He frowned. He never looked at a lady like that or had thoughts about how beautiful a lady was. What was different about Triese?

"May I pray with you, Triese? God has spoken to me and I am aware that you are in danger. Just why, He didn't say. But I would like to count you as a friend. I never walk away from a friend."

Triese stared at him. She had kept to herself since she moved to town, only going out to shop for what she needed, attend the occasional special event, and then attend the Sunday morning church service. She was in and out of anywhere she went quickly, just nodding at people. This was how she had lived her life for the past few years.

"I guess. I don't have any friends in town."

Teeg looked sad at that. He wanted to change that.

"We'll change that, Triese. My sister will want to be your friend, I can guarantee that. And so will my brother." He grinned at her for a moment, causing her to stare at the handsome man who was so concerned about her. Teeg sobered. "There were two men who appeared after I brought you here. They stayed for hours. They didn't say a word. One was inside and one outside. It was truly bizarre."

"That is strange. Where again did you find me?"

"On the other side of Willow Creek. It's running fairly wild and high right now. I saw you on the other side of the creek and managed to carry you back across the creek and then to here. You didn't rouse at all. Andy was very worried about you." He grinned down at the dog as he raised his head to look at him and then barked in agreement with Teeg's words.

"You did?" Triese frowned at him. "I don't recognize that creek."

"It's a couple of miles here and drains into the lake near town." Teeg paused, not sure how to express himself. That was totally unlike him. "I'll take you into town, Triese, and we'll see what you can remember once you're home."

"That would be nice. I feel grubby." Triese sighed. This was too much information to give a new friend, was he?

"I can only imagine that you are." He snapped his fingers. "Brit left some clothes here. She's about your size. That's my sister. She would tell you to borrow them. She's like that." Teeg was on his feet with his hand extended to her.

Triese studied his hand, studied his face, and then studied Andy. Andy stood up at her knee, a pink tongue out to lick at her face as if to say that she could trust his master. She shrugged and reached for Teeg's head. She felt happy, she decided, for the first time in years and cherished and wanted and protected. Triese had been on the run until she settled down in Red Oak. Her brother, Tait, had been looking out after her until he suddenly disappeared two years ago. She had tried to find him without any success. She missed him. Her parents knew to keep their distance as much as they wanted to be with her. Triese had decided that week that she wanted them with her. She just didn't know how to tell them that. They were all grieving Tait without knowing where he was.

Refreshed by her shower, Triese studied her face in the mirror. She frowned at her reflection before she turned to the door, gathering her dirty clothes in the plastic bag that Teeg had given her. She was grateful for the clean clothes but somewhat uncomfortable at borrowing clothes. She looked up at Teeg, wondering at his height.

"Feeling better?" Teeg grinned at her. "We can leave at any time that you're ready to."

"Thank you, Teeg. You have gone above and beyond for a stranger." Triese bit her lip as she stared up at him. She was tall for a lady but he seemed to loom over her. She was not afraid of him, unlike other men who would have been like this. "I am not afraid with you. Why?"

"God. He has been here for you, Triese. I was not planning on heading for Willow Creek yesterday.

In fact, I should have been heading the opposite direction. God sent me that way. I don't know what would have happened to you if I had not gone there." Teeg shouldered her camera bag, called for Andy and waited for Triese to exit the cabin. He locked the door behind them and then reached for her hand. Triese stared at him for a moment before she shrugged and felt his hand tighten on hers.

Chapter 4

Walking away from his cabin, Teeg was worried. He kept watch as did Andy. Andy was not alerting to anything, which somewhat relieved Teeg's mind but he knew that the men would likely return. What did they want from Triese? That was a worry as well. Teeg stared down at the lady who walked beside him, a frown on his face before it cleared. He was doing God's work, worrying about a new friend. He began to pray that God would surround Triese with His band of angels and be her Shield and Protector. He couldn't be that, as much as he suddenly desired to do so.

Triese kept pace with Teeg. She was deeply worried as well. She had no idea how she had ended up on the other side of Willow Creek and didn't know if she ever would. The fact that this had happened caused her to draw in a deep breath.

"Teeg? What is on the other side of Willow Creek?" Triese waited for Teeg to speak.

"The other side of the creek? Forest land. There are some streams as well as a bluff. Why?"

"I need to understand why I was there. I don't remember receiving any call to photograph anything near there. I would remember that." She felt in her pocket. "I have my phone. That would have my schedule on it."

Teeg nodded. He knew that she had as she had shown it to him.

“Wait until we’re in the truck. That way, you’re not distracted by anything.” Teeg reached to unlock the garage and then the truck. Opening the passenger door, he laughed as Andy charged in ahead of Triese and launched himself into the backseat.

Triese stared at Andy before she allowed Teeg to help her into the truck. Her seatbelt was fastened and she waited somewhat impatiently for him to climb behind the wheel.

Teeg pulled away from the garage, leaving it locked tightly behind him. He searched the area around him, not seeing anything that alarmed him. Hitting the highway, he headed into Red Oak, waiting patiently for Triese to search through her contacts and bookings on her phone.

“I don’t see anything that asked me to go there. I have a flight out to Northern Ontario in a month for two days. Other than that, I am home and working on my website and the photos that I have taken. I don’t travel as much as I used to.” Triese bit at her lip again, a habit that was new to her. “I don’t understand this at all, Teeg. Do you?”

“No, I don’t, Triese.” Teeg pulled into a parking lot at a coffee shop. He twisted in his seat to watch her, an amused look in his eyes as he saw that Andy was standing with his front feet on the centre console and his chin on Triese’s shoulder. “What can I do to help?”

“You’ve done more than enough. I can take it from here.” She pointed towards the road. “You need to take me home.”

"And I will do that." Teeg drove away, heading for the street that she lived on before he slowed and then pulled over to the curb. He frowned harder as he saw the police vehicles near the house where Triese said she lived and then the police tape around her lawn. His hand landed on Triese's arm to keep her in the truck. "Stay put. I'll find out what's going on. My brother is on the force and they know me." He jumped down, frowning once more as Triese appeared beside him. "Didn't I just tell you to stay put?"

"You did. This is my home. I need to talk to them myself. Don't you get that?" Triese's face had a fierce look, causing Teeg to bite back a smile. "And I see that smile. This is not funny."

"No, it's not. Nothing that you have gone through in the last few days has been funny. We'll talk with them and then you will need to be assessed at the hospital. That's not an option, Triese. You were unconscious for at least twelve hours. We need to know that there isn't something sinister in that." Teeg was adamant about that, simply staring back with a blank look on his face as she glared up at him. He felt Andy nudging his hand and rubbed at the dog's ears.

Toby Callahan turned from where he was standing at his vehicle, making notes. He was one of the three detectives on the force. He was not expecting to see his brother near the crime scene. He tucked away his notepad and pen and walked towards his brother.

"Teeg?" Toby stopped, a frown on his face as he saw his brother holding the hand of a beautiful lady. He greeted Andy almost in an absentminded manner.

"Toby? What's going on? This is Triese Cameron, who lives in the house that's blocked off." Teeg waited patiently for Toby to react.

Toby turned to Triese, studying her. He could not understand how Teeg was with her. He also didn't understand the destruction in her home. It was not what he had expected to find, knowing her line of work.

"Miss Cameron?" Toby's voice brought Triese's attention to her. "May I ask where you have been overnight?"

Triese bit at her lip once more. It was frustrating to find her home blocked off but it was also frustrating that she had not been home when this had happened.

"Me? I was unconscious at Teeg's cabin. Why?"

"It's always what we ask, Miss Cameron. And just why were you at my brother's cabin?" Toby was puzzled by that. He knew that his brother treated ladies well and would not take advantage of any lady. He also knew that his brother was not dating anyone.

"I found her on the other side of Willow Creek, Toby. She has no idea why she was there. She was unconscious when I found her and I didn't want to bring her into town. In fact, I couldn't. Not long after I got her back to my cabin, two men appeared. I was forced to sit in a chair for hours. One man stayed inside while the other man was outside. It was early evening when they disappeared. I have no idea who they were. They never said a word. I know that they checked on

Triese at different times over the day. I wasn't allowed to move. Andy stayed at my side. He was not happy."

"No, he would not be. He's very protective of you and whoever is with you." Toby turned his attention to Triese. "May I call you Triese?" At her nod, Toby turned for a moment to look at her home. "What can you tell me about your work?"

"I'm a wildlife photographer. I do travel for work but haven't had to do so for a couple of months." Triese frowned at her home. "What happened here?"

"Someone broke in overnight. Your neighbour was concerned when he saw the front door open and couldn't get any response from you. We've been through it. A lot of stuff has been tossed around as we say. The crime scene techs are almost done and then we'll walk through your home. And yes, Teeg and Andy can come with you." Toby walked away with a smirk on his face as he heard her outreached voice stating that wasn't necessary. It was very necessary, Toby knew. Teeg was not going to allow her to walk into that mess on his own. His phone was out as he called for their sister to head their way. Brit didn't ask why, just stated that she would.

Chapter 5

Teeg reached for Triese's hand as Toby beckoned them forward. Toby held the police tape up for them to duck under. Andy paced beside Teeg's side. He had gone into work mode. Teeg and Andy were a team with the search and rescue group and the dog could sense that something was wrong. Triese's steps paused as a hand came to cover her mouth to prevent her from crying out as she saw the damage on her front porch.

Teeg's hand tightened on Triese's as he waited for her to move forward. It took her some moments to compose herself. Andy leaned against her, trying his best to bring comfort to her. Triese finally moved a foot to walk forward. Teeg prayed aloud for her as they walked into the house. Tears were near the surface as she paced from room to room, seeing the damage and destruction.

"I don't understand, Toby. I really don't understand. Who would do this?" Triese was terrified at the thought that someone had been in her home and had done this destruction. She slumped into a chair in the kitchen, burying her face in her hands. An arm went out to hug Andy as he stood up to lick at the tears on her cheeks.

"I don't understand either, Triese. I'm off duty now. Brit is outside. We'll help you to clean up the mess and get your home back to as much as normal as it can be." Toby's hand landed on his brother's shoulder as he walked past him.

Teeg was kneeling beside her, an arm around her. He didn't say anything. He didn't have the words to say. Instead, he prayed for her, asking for God's protection on her.

Triese rose at last and walked back through her home. She was determined to find out who had done this and find it out that day. She sighed to herself. This was not how she had planned her weekend. She had wanted to go away and find somewhere she could just commune with her Heavenly Father. This was not happening.

Brit stopped by Teeg before hugging him. She was as puzzled as Toby had been when she found Teeg with Triese.

"Teeg?"

"Brit. Thanks for coming. Triese needs a friend and you might just be the right person." Teeg briefly explained what had transpired over the past hours.

"You found her? God led you there, didn't he?" Brit turned as she heard Triese returning. "Introduce me to your lady, brother."

Teeg stared at her. Just what had she meant? He had no lady, not yet anyway. It was a prayer of his to find his lady and spend the rest of his life with her. She just had not appeared yet, or had she? He shook his head at the nudge from God.

"Triese? This brat is my sister, Brit. She's here to help clean up your home."

Triese was surprised at the hug Brit gave her before the other lady stepped back and looked around.

"Teeg? We'll need some of those oversize contractor garbage bags. You have some in your truck?"

"I do." Teeg was away and moving his truck closer. He waited for Toby to catch up with him.

Toby had disappeared to his home and changed to casual clothing. He walked towards his brother, helping to take down the police tape.

"Teeg? What do you know about Triese?"

"Not a lot. She didn't say much. She was unconscious until this morning." Teeg rubbed at his cheek. "She doesn't remember getting to Willow Creek. She has no idea who the men were. This is a mystery." Teeg stared down at the ground. "How do we do this?"

"We don't. I do. It's an investigation that will take time. To be honest with you, there was not a lot of evidence recovered." Toby walked into the house, finding Triese waiting for him. "Triese?"

"You said that there wasn't much evidence? How do we find them? Is this why I've been running for years?" Triese was sober. "My parents live near Ottawa. I have a brother who I have not seen in two years. Tait just disappeared. We can't find him, no matter how we try. Dad even hired a private investigator who charged him a lot and did nothing." She felt Teeg's arm around her and leaned against him. This was not something that she usually shared so quickly if at all.

“He did? Let me have all the information, Triese. I’ll look into it. It may be related to what you’ve been through.” He looked around. “For now, let us help you restore your home. Anything that is broken, we’ll set aside. You’ll need to reach out to your insurance agent.”

“I left a voice mail for him. He’ll call me back on Monday, likely. As long as we have photos of everything, we should be okay.” She reached for her camera. “I guess that’s my job, isn’t it?” Triese walked away, a sober look on her face.

“She’s hurting in many ways, Teeg. Be careful with her.” Toby headed for the living room, asking Brit where they were starting.

Three hours later, the house was restored as much as they could do it. Bags of broken and damaged items were dropped in the box of Teeg’s truck. Toby had disappeared near the end of their struggle to clean up her home and returned with a meal for them all. Triese had hugged him for that thoughtfulness, tears near the surface. She had not expected the three of them to give up their day to help her. She had been prepared to do it on her own.

Brit watched her closely. They had had a chance to talk over the day and even shared laughter at times. Triese was someone who Brit wanted to know better and she already considered her a friend.

“We’ve done what we can today, Triese. You need to repaint some of the rooms. We’ll look after that next week.” Teeg looked up at she made a sound.

"We're not letting you do that on your own. And Toby wants to talk to you about a security system."

"I know. I keep putting it off and shouldn't." Triese didn't want to take that step but knew that she had to.

"It's tough to make that decision. We see it all the time." Toby was compassionate in his tone of voice. "Where do you store your backups?"

"My backups? For the computer?" At Toby's nod, Triese drew in a deep breath. "I have a safe that is well hidden. No one can find it. That's where the backups go. I put them away every day. And I think that is good that I do. They couldn't find them and couldn't access my computer. Were they after photos, do you think?" Her question caused the other three to pause and stare at her before Toby was nodding. That had been one of the first things that he had considered when he found out Triese's occupation.

Chapter 6

Triese stood for a moment with her back to the front door. She felt violated and unsafe in her own home. The destruction that she had faced? It had tested her strength in more ways than one. To have had Teeg and his family there had helped. Brit had expressed a wish to meet with her for Bible study and prayer. Triese had stared at her before she had nodded. She had no friends, not really, in Red Oak. Brit's offer of friendship had been a welcome gift.

Staring at the damaged walls, Triese felt fear once more. She turned off the lights as she walked back through the house, heading for her bedroom. She was exhausted and needed to rest. Teeg had tried his best to get her to go to the hospital but she had refused. Her feeling was that if she had been drugged and that seemed likely from what Toby had said, the drugs would no longer be in her system. That worried her. She had no memory of how she had disappeared from her home.

Teeg had walked away from Triese, deeply troubled by the fact that she was on her own against an unknown enemy. She could not explain what had happened. He had talked long with Toby about it and his brother had not been able to give much information as to what she was facing. There was just not enough information to explain what had happened or why or who. Andy had been reluctant to leave Triese. Teeg had had to literally pick up the dog and carry him to his truck. He had smiled sadly at that. He had to admit that he felt the same way.

Driving home, Teeg was watchful. Toby had warned him about being careful and to be well aware of who was around him. He was a target now just because he stepped in and helped Triese despite not knowing why that was. He thought back through the day before and the two men before shaking his head. He did not know them.

Andy jumped from the truck as Teeg parked near his cabin. Parking there was something he did at times. Tonight was one of those times. Andy was searching around the cabin, his hackles raised. Teeg watched him before shaking his head. Someone or something had been around. He headed for the back door, unlocking it and stepping inside. He reached to turn off his security system. Toby had been adamant when Teeg had taken over the cabin that he set up such a system. Tonight, he was glad that he had.

Andy rushed by him, searching in the cabin before he came back to sit in front of Teeg. His owner dropped to his knees and wrapped the dog in a hug, knowing that both of them were missing Triese. How had she become so important to them in such a short period of time?

Early the next morning, Teeg was searching outside of his home. Andy was still edgy and upset when he was outside. He nodded as he pulled cameras from their hiding places. This must have been what the one man had done when he was outside of his cabin two days ago. He dropped them into a plastic bag and set it on his kitchen table. These would go to Toby that morning. He turned to lock his door, leaving Andy at home despite the dog's protests. He unlocked his truck, pausing for a moment, before he drove off. He was headed for Triese despite her protest that she could drive herself.

Triese stared at Teeg as he grinned at her. She had answered her door, a piece of toast in her hand. She stepped back to let him enter.

"I told you that I would drive myself." Triese was disgruntled and it showed.

"I know that you did. You can't. Toby wants one of the mechanics to go over your vehicle." Teeg didn't say what Toby had told him.

"He does? Why?" Triese waited for him to respond. "Teeg? Why ?"

"Because your car may have been tampered with during whatever it was that happened. They seem to want to harm you for some reason. That reason we need to figure out." Triese's hand on his arm stopped Teeg.

"My car?" Triese paled. "They would do that?"

"I think that they would. He'll make sure that it's fine. Roger is one of the best mechanics we both know. If something is wrong, he'll find it. He'll be at church this morning."

"And just where is Andy?" She changed the topic.

"He's at home. It's too warm for him to be in the truck and I don't take him into the church, even though he is welcome." Teeg paced the hallway from the front door to the kitchen and back. "We should get underway soon."

Triese dropped the toast that she no longer wanted into the organics bin before she washed her hands and then reached for her purse and Bible. She watched Teeg as he stared out of the front door window. An image of him doing this for the rest of their lives startled and shook her. Triese was not planning on marrying anyone. This was a battle that she was continually going back to God with. Perhaps she needed to change her thoughts.

Teeg seated Triese in a pew near the back of the church, Brit sliding in beside them. He knew that Toby was around. He had seen his truck in the parking lot. He stood for a moment before he shook his head and sat, his arm brushing against Triese.

That afternoon, Triese stood with her arms folded across her abdomen, her eyes on Roger as he worked around her car. He had not let her remove it from the garage, simply stating that he wanted to go over it first before they moved the car. He was frowning as he slid underneath it. Back out, he beckoned for Toby to approach. Roger was disturbed, Toby could tell. A few moments of quiet conversation between the two men had Triese frowning at them.

Toby turned to walk towards Triese, noting that Teeg was standing as close to the lady as he could. He nodded to himself. There was interest there, he decided.

"Triese? We need to tow your car to a garage. The brake lines have been punctured. Roger wants to go over it better once it's up on a hoist. We don't know if there is any other damage." Toby was angry. He had no idea why she had been targeted like this but he wanted answers, answers that he not likely would get for some time. The men who had ransacked her home and damaged her vehicle had done this to a friend of his brother's and that didn't sit right with him.

"There are?" Triese shrank back, finding Teeg's arms around her to keep her upright. "Who? Why? I don't have any enemies. I'm a wildlife photographer. I work with nature, not people." She was almost in tears.

"We'll figure it out, Triese." Teeg shared a long look with his brother. A lady that he was interested in was threatened and that meant Teeg would step in to help her without any thought of his own safety.

Chapter 7

Triese stood in her office late that afternoon. She had had to finally send Teeg away. He had been reluctant to leave her, insisting that he needed to protect her. She had frowned at him before she had walked him to the door and sent him on his way. Triese smiled at how he had tried to care for her. She was not used to that. Triese had been standing on her own two feet since she was a teenager. Her family had backed her on that. Her brother had been her most staunch defender, vocal in how he supported her. Triese missed Tait at that moment. She needed her brother and he wasn't there.

Teeg found his favourite chair in his backyard. Andy dropped down to cover his feet, his nose on his paws. Teeg watched him, knowing that he was missing Triese despite the brief time that he had known her.

"I know, buddy. I know. I want to be with Triese as well. We can't. And we have work in the morning. We can't find her until tomorrow night. And we will." Teeg was content just to sit in God's nature and spend time in prayer. He was begging God to be Triese's shield and protector at this time. He wanted to be that but had no right. He didn't dismiss the interest that he felt but knew that it had to be God's timing and not his.

Late the next afternoon, Teeg dropped his backpack beside his desk, stretching as he did so. His walking stick was set by the back door as it usually was. Andy had headed for his water bowl and then to pace the house. Teeg frowned at him, sensing that someone had been around that day. He sat at his desk, pulling up the security feed. It was as he had thought. The two men had been back around over the day, trying to gain entry to his cabin. He copied the feed and forwarded it to Toby. Toby was back to him in just moments, asking if these were the men from Friday. Teeg responded in the positive before he was on his feet and heading for a shower and clean clothes.

Glancing at his watch as he headed into town, Teeg headed for a local diner to pick up a meal before he turned towards Triese's house. He prayed that he was not overstepping his bounds in doing so. Andy waited impatiently as Teeg parked in front of the house before he was out of the truck and running for the door, a delighted bark coming from him.

Triese frowned as she plugged in the kettle. She was hearing a dog barking that sounded at her front door. She didn't know any dog in the neighbourhood that would do it. She walked that way, frowning still as she stared out of the front door. Yes, he just had to show up and with a meal.

"Teeg? Didn't you just leave?" Triese's smile lit up her face as she rubbed at Andy. The dog had jumped up to wash her face.

"It's been a day, Triese. I brought a meal." Teeg grinned as he held up the bag of food.

"Food? Then, come in. I'm starved and was just about to make a sandwich. This sounds much better." Triese headed for the kitchen. "And you are welcome here." She stared down at the dog. "What about Andy?"

"He's eaten already before we left home." Teeg reached to hug her, finding her returning the hug.

This seemed to become a habit that week. Teeg would show up with a meal or Triese would have something ready for them. Their conversations were varied, sometimes very animated.

Saturday found Teeg turning from his cabin door and reaching for Triese's hand. She had insisted on seeing just where he had found her. He could not deny her that. He had had a long conversation with Toby who had appeared mid-week and asked to see the same area. Toby had been open with his brother, knowing that Triese would have talked with him. Her car had been damaged more that they thought and it would take time to repair. She had been angry and Toby had to say that he didn't blame her. He would have been angry as well.

Triese was apprehensive, she had to admit. She had been awake really early that morning, needing to pray through what she was doing that day. God had given her peace but she still was uncertain as to the steps that she was walking. Teeg's grip on her hand was comforting as was Andy's presence.

Stopping at last, Triese stared at Willow Creek. It was not as high or as wild as it had been the week before but it was still higher than she expected. She turned to Teeg and found him watching her. Andy ran across the log without any difficulty. Triese was not sure that she could do that.

“You want me to walk over that?” Her finger pointed at the log even as her voice held her disbelief.

“I do. It’s okay. Just let me hold your hand.” Teeg grinned at her.

“Not a chance, buster. I’ll make it over on my own.” Triese tentatively set her foot on the log, her arms extended out from her sides for balance.

Teeg waited patiently for Triese to make her way over to the other side before he carefully made his way across. He reached to hug her, not surprising her with his actions. She was becoming accustomed to his hugs and in fact, had admitted to herself that she was looking forward to them. Triese was puzzled at that.

Teeg grinned at her before he looked around. He pointed off to one side.

“That’s where I found you. You were unconscious and I had to carry you across the log.”

Triese stared at him, horror on her face for a moment. She spun to stare at the log and then at the creek.

“It was higher last week?” Her question ended in a squeak.

“It was. It’s okay. I managed to get you across and to safety. Now, we need to figure out why you were here. And your camera case was with you.”

Triese frowned at him, thinking through the previous week. She shook her head, not sure what to say.

“I don’t remember Friday at all. I remember going to bed Thursday night. My plans were to work on photos that I wanted to print and then frame. Apparently, that didn’t happen. I have no idea what happened. Is that normal?”

“It can be. We shut down in times of danger. And that is likely what happened to you. Has Toby said anything about what they found?”

Triese shook her head. Toby had spoken with her the night before. There wasn’t a lot that he could tell her. Her car had been returned to her, repaired at no cost by Roger. He had been that concerned about her. She was both puzzled and worried about what was happening. And it didn’t help that it now concerned Teeg and his family.

Chapter 8

Triese walked around the area, not sure what she was to be looking for. Andy paced beside her, alert but not reacting to anything. Teeg paced away from them, searching himself. He had no idea what had caused Triese to be left out here on her own and unconscious at that.

Turning to watch Triese and Andy, Teeg gave a small smile. He was hurting for her with the uncertainty of what had happened. To have her car damaged as well was unexpected. He had taken time to speak with Roger and had been shocked at the damage that had been done. Someone wanted Triese to die and it didn't seem to matter in what manner that happened. He looked up, saying a prayer for her.

The breeze was beginning to pick up as clouds began to cover the blue sky. Teeg looked up, suddenly aware of the change in the weather. He ran towards Triese, catching her hand and tugging her towards the woods nearby, desperately searching for shelter. A small cave caught his eye and he pulled Triese into it. Andy shot ahead of them, turning to almost lay on Triese's knees. He crouched down in front of her, sideways so that he could watch Triese and Andy.

"Teeg? What was that all bout?"

"A storm is moving in and we needed to find shelter." Teeg ducked his head to stare at the sky. It was as he thought. It was a brutal storm moving in and who knew when they would be able to head home.

And there was the problem of crossing the creek. If it rained too much, the creek would rise to cover the log.

"Teeg? Couldn't we have just headed back to your cabin?"

"No. We would not have made it. We'll be fine here." Teeg grinned at her, praying that his words would be correct.

Three hours later, they stepped out into the soaked clearing, their shoes and jean legs soaking up the water. Teeg was afraid. There had been such a violent downpour with lightning and thunder that didn't seem to stop. He headed them towards the creek, his steps slowing as he saw what he had feared. The log was covered with water and from experience, he knew that it would take time to recede. There was no way that they could make it across safely. The only other crossing was miles up the creek and would be in the same condition.

"Teeg? We can't cross that. How do we get to the other side?" Triese spun in a circle, desperate to find a way to do that.

"I know, Triese. I know. We can walk down the creek to the lake and then hopefully get a ride around the lake. I just don't know if we can make it before dark." Triese reached to wrap an arm around her. "I'll get you home."

"I know you will. I just don't like being out here in the open." Triese shrugged off his arm and started walking along the bank of the creek. She was determined to make it to the lake before dark. She just didn't know if they would make it.

Teeg's head dropped for a moment before he ran to catch up with her. His hand reached for hers, the warmth of it bringing comfort to Triese. Andy surged ahead, determined to lead his people to safety.

Hours later, they paused at the mouth of the creek, staring at the lake and then at one another. Teeg pointed to the left, heading that way. He knew the couple that lived in the house that was visible, who were fellow churchgoers. He tapped at their door, waiting for Ted to answer.

Ted stared at them for a moment before he beckoned them in.

"Teeg? What are you doing here? And who is this with you?"

"This is Triese Cameron. We were caught on this side of Willow Creek by the storm. Any chance that we could get a lift into town?"

"Not a problem. Come and sit. We'll have a coffee first. You've been walking for hours." Ted reached for the coffee pot and poured them coffee, finding the tin of squares that Mary had tucked in a cupboard. "Sit. Drink your coffee and have some squares. Mary's off at a meeting."

Thirty minutes later, Teeg and Triese were dropped off at his cabin. Andy immediately began searching around the area, his hackles raised. Waving Ted off, Teeg turned and paused as he watched his dog. He reached for the truck door, his hand dropping before he touched it. There was no way that Teeg could touch his vehicle.

Triese stared at him and then at the truck. She frowned at the truck. Something was off about it but she didn't know what. She was just not that familiar with it.

"Teeg? What's wrong with your truck? Aren't we heading into town?"

Teeg shook his head before he tucked Triese onto his front porch and then walked around his vehicle. Dropping to his knees, he studied the ground underneath the truck. He frowned and then was back on his feet, reaching for his phone. Toby was not happy to hear that Teeg's truck had been tampered with.

Walking slowly back to the cabin, Teeg rubbed at his cheek. His eyes were on Triese, who was watching him with apprehension on her face.

"Teeg? Your truck?"

"Someone has tampered with it. I'm sorry. I'm not able to drive you home. Toby is on his way."

"Okay. Can I go inside? I can find us a meal, I think, if you'll let me." Triese walked into the cabin, studying it with fresh eyes. She really didn't remember it.

"Just help yourself to whatever looks good. I'll look after Andy." Teeg walked back outside, more disturbed than he wanted Triese to know. He looked around before he walked the perimeter of his property. Andy ran towards him, standing up at him to be loved on. "Someone was here, weren't they, Andy? You know that and recognize the men, don't you? I can tell."

Andy gave a low woof and ran away, heading for where Triese stood watching them. Teeg lifted a hand to her before he continued his inspection. The men seemed to have spent some time there. He turned to study the cabin, knowing that they would not have been able to get in. He had seen to that.

Chapter 9

Toby walked around his brother's cabin, staying out of the way of the crime scene techs. Roger, he knew, was working on the truck, muttering away to himself. This is not how he expected his Saturday to end. He was on call until midnight and had prayed for a quiet evening. That had not happened.

"Toby? What are your thoughts?" Teeg approached his brother, Triese beside him. Toby had noticed that wherever Teeg was that evening, Triese was with him. He smiled thoughtfully at that.

"That whoever it was has come back. It was likely the men from a week ago. What are they after?" Toby frowned at Triese who was staring back at him, a shuttered look on her face. "Triese? Remembered anything since we last talked?"

"Not a thing. We were back there but the storm moved in before we had a chance to look around much. That means we need to go back there." Triese frowned at the two men as their heads were shaking. "Yes, we do. I need to see that area in more detail." She walked away, Andy at her side, his protective nature very much in evidence.

"She's going to head back there, you know, Teeg?" Toby grinned at his brother.

"I know. And she will head out there on her own unless we prevent it." Teeg sighed. "I have to be out in the forest next week. I have no choice. And that's just when she'll decide to go out there. And we can't stop her."

"No, we can't. I'll talk to Brit. She would be good to go with her." Brit had taken up martial arts in her teens and was now a trainer in that. "I'm sure that she'll be agreeable to go with her if you're not available." Toby turned as he heard footsteps. "Roger?"

Roger stalked towards the two men, anger on his face. This was rare for him. He usually didn't show his anger, not like this. Triese crowded close to Teeg once more, finding his hand reaching for hers. Andy growled at Roger, upset at the anger that he sensed.

"Roger?" Toby repeated his question, sharing a look with his brother.

"Teeg? Who did you anger? Or is it Triese?" Roger pointed towards Teeg's truck. "There's a bomb underneath it, caught up in the brakes. If you had taken off, then you would have set off the bomb and likely died. So, who did you anger?"

The three stared at Roger in shock, Triese whimpering for a moment with the intenseness of her emotions.

"I have no idea, Roger. I don't make any enemies. At least, I don't think I do. The only men would be the ones that threatened Triese."

"I have no idea who they were. I never saw them." Triese wrinkled her brow. "Teeg? You never did describe them to me. How am I to avoid them if I don't know what they look like?" She was angry at

Teeg for a moment and then at the circumstances that had brought them together. She was also very afraid and just wanted her family.

"We'll discuss that, Triese." Toby was adamant about that. "But first, we need to deal with this. Roger? You called it in?"

"I did. Ed and his team will be here shortly. He asked that we move somewhere safe. Just where would that be?" Roger looked around for somewhere they could wait for Ed and his team.

"Let's head to the back of the cabin. It is sheltered there." Teeg was exhausted. It had been a long day already and it wasn't ending anytime soon. He tugged Triese with him through the house, pausing as he did so to grab some food and bottles of water for them all. Triese reached to help him before grabbing Andy's food bowl. Teeg gave her a tight smile before he nodded towards the door.

Toby reached to help them. Roger was still waiting near the truck for Ed and his team. Both the officers were angry, Toby more so as it was his brother involved. And then there was Triese. He could see the interest that both of them were trying hard to hide. He had waited for years for Teeg to be interested in a lady. He had prayed that it would not be because of danger but God had other plans, it would seem.

Ed walked around the cabin an hour later, a device in an evidence bag. He stopped as he saw Toby, Triese, and Teeg just sitting and not talking. He hesitated to approach them but Andy had seen him and rose to come towards him. He knew Ed and greeted him as he would a friend.

Toby looked around and then waved Ed towards them. Ed sat, his eyes on the bag before he looked up. Teeg was watching him closely, waiting patiently for Ed to speak. This was something that he had learned over time with his work.

"Ed? What do you have?" Toby reached for the bag, tilting it to study the bomb. "Rather amateurish, isn't it?"

"It is but it would have been effective." Ed stared at Toby for a moment before his attention shifted to Teeg. "Teeg? What have you gone and done?"

Teeg shrugged. As far as he knew, he had done nothing. There had been instances where he had had to call in the authorities.

"I have no idea, Ed. All I did was find Triese and rescue her." He looked down at her. "Let's have a seat and try and figure it out if we can."

Ed nodded, reaching to pull a chair out from the table and sat, his eyes thoughtful. He knew Teeg and knew that he would have gone to Toby or someone else if he had needed to. He watched Triese in turn, a frown on his face. Ed was sure that he knew her from somewhere. He just didn't know where.

A sudden yell had the men on their feet, spinning to face towards the forest. The team member, John, was running towards them.

“Run. Head away from here. I just found another bomb.” John raced towards them, fear on his face. That was unusual for the seasoned officer.

Teeg grabbed for Triese’s hand and turned to run. Only, they never made it very far from where they had been seated. The explosion rocked the air, sending them flying forward to land on the ground and not move. Teeg had wrapped Triese in his arms as they headed for the ground, turning his body to take the brunt of the fall, praying as he did that he could protect her.

Andy ran towards his master, sniffing at him and then on his belly, trying to rouse Teeg. He pawed at him and then his tongue was out washing at both Teeg and Triese. They didn’t respond. Andy had been exploring the forest when the bomb went off and was saved from harm. He finally gave up trying to rouse Teeg and just cuddled close to him, a chin on his arm.

Chapter 10

Debris and smoke floated through the air, silence now the most prominent part of the afternoon. The forest critters had been quieted by the violence of the explosion. They gradually began to peek out and then move around. It felt as if hours had passed while it had only been minutes. A brave squirrel moved towards the bodies on the ground, stopping to sit up and study them before he bounded past them and to safety. He paused once more to sniff at the air, not likely the smell of the explosion.

None of the bodies moved. Andy rose at last, nosing each of the men and then Triese before his head went back and he howled. He wanted his master to calm him but that was not happening.

Brit parked near her brother's garage, puzzled at the police vehicle that was parked there. Fear suddenly hit her and she began to run for her brother's cabin. Brit slid to a stop, horror on her face as she saw the destruction from the bomb. She searched frantically for Teeg even as her phone was out to call for help.

"Teeg? Teeg?" Brit's voice grew louder and more frantic as she searched for her brother. She had no idea that both of her brothers were present and lying unconscious from the force of the blast.

Her feet picked up their speed as she raced around the house, still calling for Teeg. She slid to an abrupt halt as she saw the bodies, a scream wrenched from her body. Andy raced towards her, barking wildly, jumping up at her before he ran back towards his master and his lady.

Brit's phone was out as she frantically called for help before she ran for Teeg. She once more slid to a stop as she stared at Toby. What was going on? She had no idea. Brit was on her knees beside Toby, a hand to his chest. She breathed with relief as she felt his heart beat.

Looking around, Brit's eyes. Narrowed as she saw Ed and John as well. On her way past, she ensured that they were still alive. Her knees hurt as she dropped to her knees beside Teeg. She was worried about him but a slight smile crossed her face as she saw how Teeg and Triese were holding tight to one another. She felt for pulses before Andy nudged inbetween her and Teeg. She could tell that Andy was worried about his master and his lady.

A hand on her shoulder caused her to scream even as she spun and stared up at the police chief.

"Uncle Tyler?" Brit was lifted to her feet and moved away from the patients as paramedics moved in. "What are you doing here?"

"I'm here because this is a crime scene. And you're family." He drew Brit further away and stood with an arm around his niece.

"What happened, Uncle Ty?"

"There was a bomb on Teeg's truck. Toby found it and called in Ed and John. Roger was here but left. He'll be back shortly." Tyler Callahan was deeply worried about his two nephews as well as the other officers. This was not something that had ever happened that he was aware of. And it just had to be his family.

Brit moved away from her uncle, a thoughtful look on her face as she paced where she could before she stood and stared at Toby. He was sitting up and speaking, not willing to be transported to the hospital. His eyes met hers as she frowned at him.

"Toby? You're going in. There is nothing that you can say that will stop that." Brit was stern with her brother, knowing that he wouldn't go if she wasn't.

Toby nodded and regretted it, the headache getting worse.

"I guess I have to." His eyes were somewhat blurry as he looked around. His focus centred on Teeg. "Teeg? Triese?"

"They're still unconscious, Toby." Ty had moved close to his nephew. "They're ready to transport some of you. They're still working on Teeg and Triese." Ty didn't continue. He couldn't. He was worried about his nephew and his lady but he had other duties that needed his attention. "Brit? Let me have your keys. You can ride with Toby."

Brit nodded, her keys handed over. She frowned at Andy who was showing his distress.

"What about Andy?"

"I'll look after him." Ty studied the cabin. "I'll have someone come out and board up the windows and then have someone come through and clean up the place." He had been inside and was dismayed at the damage that had been done.

"I see." Brit hugged her uncle and then walked away, heading for the paramedic rig where she knew that she would find Toby. She slipped into the cab, her head turning to watch her brother and also Ed.

Ty walked over to where to where the paramedics were still working on Teeg and Triese. Triese was ready to transport, he could tell, even though she had not regained consciousness. Teeg was talking but from his slurred words and difficulty framing answers, Ty knew that he was not doing well at the moment. He nodded as the paramedics moved away with them. He knew also that he had to track down his brother and his wife. This was one call that he didn't want to make. All he knew was that they were in Northern Ontario somewhere. He just wasn't sure where.

Brit paced the waiting room at the hospital. She wanted to be with her brothers but she had not been allowed to. She also worried about Triese. Brit had asked if she could be notified as next of kin for her as she had no one and Teeg wasn't able to do that. The nurse, a friend of hers, had nodded, knowing that Brit would not be asking that if there had been anyone at all for Brit.

Toby appeared beside his sister, wrapping an arm around her. He was sore and hurting in ways that he had never hurt before. He was told that he was fortunate not to have a concussion but he would be hurting and hurting badly in the next few days. His supervisor had been around and bluntly told him that he would not be working for the next week. He needed that time to heal.

"Toby? Should you be on your feet?" Brit studied her brother, seeing the pain in his eyes.

"I have to be. I need to find Teeg." Toby sank down gratefully into a chair, keeping an arm around his sister.

"You can't. No one is allowed there yet. I've asked but was told that I had to wait. The same for Triese." Brit bit at her lip. "What happened, Toby? Uncle Ty said something about a bomb."

"There was one. John had removed the one from the truck. Then, we heard him running towards us and yelling. That's the last I remember. I think that there might have been another bomb." He looked up as his uncle sat beside him. "Uncle Ty?"

"Toby? You okay? You're not. I can see it in your face." Ty studied Toby before he shared a look with Brit. "I've tracked down your parents. They'll head for home tonight. And don't say that I shouldn't have. They need to be here and you all need them." He sighed. "And there was a bomb that went off as well as least three others around the cabin. It is a wonder that Andy didn't set them off."

Toby paled even further at that.

"More than one? What has Teeg become involved in?" Toby's head went back against the wall as his eyes closed.

Brit watched him closely, knowing that he would want to be on his own. That was not happening.

Wherever he ended up was where she would end up. All she could do was praise God that her brothers were not dead. She had to confirm with herself that God was indeed in control.

Chapter 11

Teeg moved restlessly on the bed, his eyes narrowed at he watched Brit. She was hovering but he could not send her away. She was too worried and as an older brother, he had always taken care of her. This time, the roles were reversed and she was taking care of him. Teeg had no idea what had happened and Brit wasn't saying. The investigator was on his way to speak with Teeg. Brit had been warned not to say anything to Teeg until after that.

"Brit? Where am I?" Teeg moved again, pain wracking his whole body. "What did I do?"

"You were hurt, Teeg. I was asked not to say anything until you've given a statement. And yes, it was a crime." Brit walked from the room, seeing the investigator, Jason, approaching. "He's awake, Jason, but he is confused. I don't know that he remembers what happened."

"Thanks, Brit. Are you okay?" Jason was worried about Brit, knowing that both of her brothers had been hurt.

Brit shrugged, her eyes on a room down the hall. She walked away and headed for Triese. That lady needed someone with her and had no one. She turned as she heard a familiar voice and was enveloped in her mother's arms. Her father stood next to her, waiting his turn to hug his daughter.

Titus and Sari shared a look. It had been a long and worrying drive home. They had managed to speak with Toby, who had not been quite coherent. Their apprehension and fear had grown until they had found Tyler waiting for them.

"Ty?" Titus stared at his brother, waiting for him to speak.

"Titus? Sari?" Titus pointed towards the hospital entrance. "Toby's gone home. I have someone with him. Teeg is still here. Jason's with him at the moment. And Brit is with Triese."

The parents shared a look, puzzlement in their gazes.

"Triese? Who is she?" Sari wasn't familiar with that name.

"Triese? She's a lady that has become involved in Teeg's life or is it the other way around? He rescued her about a week ago and then they've been trying to work through what has happened. It's a story in itself. For now, let's get you to Teeg. I know that Toby plans on coming back even though he shouldn't." Tyler watched as his brother and his wife walked into Teeg's room before he turned to find Brit.

"Brit?" Tyler's voice caused his niece to jump. She spun to stare at him. "Your mom and dad are here."

"They are? Okay, I'll catch up with them in a bit." She looked back at Triese. That lady had not roused as yet. "I need to stay with Triese."

"I know that you do, but you also need to reassure your parents that you're okay. Toby's heading back here."

"That's what he said. He went home to get cleaned up. He's angry, Uncle Ty."

"And well he should be. You all should be. But I know that Teeg won't be." Or at least, that was what Tyler thought.

Brit was shaking her head. She had had a long conversation with her brother two days earlier. He was angry in a way that she had never seen before. Brit's eyes were on Triese. This was why, she decided. Having Triese in his life and in danger was driving his anger. And that he would work through, she knew.

"He is angry, Uncle Ty. And it's because of Triese."

Tyler thought through her words and nodded. Brit was reading her brother correctly. He turned slightly as he heard footsteps and found Sari reaching for her daughter.

Brit hugged her mother tighter than she had in years. She was so glad to have her parents here with them even though their vacation was cut short.

"Where's Dad?" Brit looked around for her father.

"He's with Teeg. Teeg is not doing very well, is he?" Sari was worried about her son.

"No, he's not. I don't like what happened to him or to Toby or to Triese. I don't understand it." She was frowning at Triese.

Triese had roused to some extent, hearing voices in the room. She recognized Brit's but not the others. Unable to stay still, she moved slightly and tried to find a more comfortable place to lie on. That wasn't happening. She jumped as she felt a hand on hers.

"Triese? Are you waking up?" Brit's voice held hope that she was. She had been begging God to wake up both Teeg and Triese. It seemed as if He had answered.

"Brit? Where am I?" Triese's eyes opened and closed before they stayed open. She looked around and found Brit right next to her. Her eyes then moved to stare at the lady next to Brit. "Who are you?"

"I'm Sari. I'm mother to Teeg, Toby, and Brit. I am happy to meet you but I wish that it had been under different circumstances." Sari almost shoved her daughter to one side just so that she could reach and wrap Triese in a gentle hug. "You need a mother and I gather that yours isn't here."

Triese sniffed as she felt the mother's arms around her. She missed her mother and just needed her.

"Thank you. Mom isn't here and I need her." Triese shifted back on her pillow, staring around the room. "What happened?"

"A bomb went off at Teeg's. You were all knocked out." Tyler spoke from where he stood at the end of her bed. "I'm Tyler Callahan, uncle to those three, but I am also the police chief. We'll need to have Jason take your statement or what you can remember. Brit? Sari?"

The two ladies nodded and left, leaving Tyler studying Triese.

"Triese? How are you feeling?"

Triese shrugged, not sure how she felt.

"I don't know how I'm supposed to feel. I have no memory of what happened. And you want me to tell you what I can remember." Her voice had risen to some extent as she spoke, Jason watching from beside her.

"Triese? I'm Jason. I'm here to get your statement. But it doesn't sound as if you have much of one to give."

"No, I don't remember anything." Her eyes closed and she slept.

Jason and Tyler exchanged a glance before Jason walked away. He nodded at the officer who was standing just outside of her door. Until they could find any evidence to say that Triese was safe in the hospital, a guard would be there.

Chapter 12

Teeg shifted his head restlessly on his pillow. He was due to be discharged soon but he didn't want to leave. There was someone who he needed to protect. He just didn't remember who it was. Convinced that the lady was here in the hospital as well, Teeg shoved aside the blankets and swung his legs over the edge of the bed. He had to wait until the vertigo eased before he was off the bed and reaching for the clothes that Brit had brought him.

Heading for the hallway, Teeg paused. He had no idea where he was to go but he spied the officer standing outside a room just down the hall from where he was standing. He walked that way, a hand out to trace along the wall to help him balance himself.

"In there, Teeg. Triese is awake." The officer smiled kindly at him as he pushed open the door.

Triese looked up from where she was standing at the window, contemplating the sky. She was dressed, just waiting for Brit to return for her.

"Teeg?" Triese flew across the room, stopping abruptly as she reached him. "You're on your feet?"

"I am. You're Triese? I'm sorry. I have a memory problem right now." Teeg reached out to touch her cheek.

"I am." She frowned at him.

“I’m sorry. You’re a beautiful lady. I would like to date you.” Teeg wasn’t aware of what he was saying.

Triese remembered at last to snap her mouth closed. Was he for real? Triese wasn’t sure that he even knew what he was asking.

“Teeg? What did you just ask me?”

Teeg looked at her with a puzzled look on his face. He didn’t remember what he said. All he knew was that he didn’t want to let this lady out of his sight.

“What did I say? I can’t remember.”

“Teeg!” Triese’s wail was low. She stared at him, not sure that he was for real.

“You said that you wanted to date me.”

“I did? Then, I guess that I do. Will you go out with me?” Teeg reached to hug her, staggering slightly as he did so. He hurt, all over, and his head was starting to ache in a harder manner.

“Teeg? Off your feet.” Triese gently shoved him into a chair and then sat across from him. “You need to be in bed.”

Teeg eyed her, wanting to shake his head but knowing that he couldn’t.

“I mean that, I guess. You need to tell me what we were doing.”

Triese stared at him before she sighed. She told him everything that had happened, seeing the disbelief and the resignation on his face.

"How badly was my home damaged?"

"I don't know. That hasn't been a priority for me." Triese sat back, her arms folded across her abdomen. "Someone else will need to tell you that."

Teeg nodded, a sigh rising in his chest. He wanted to go home but it sounded as if he would not be able to. He didn't want to move to his parents. His mother would hover and he didn't want that. That left either Toby or Brit. He would choose Brit, he decided, knowing that Toby had also been injured.

"I do mean it, Triese. I don't know why we're together but I don't want to lose you as a friend."

"I get that. But right now, neither of us are ready for this. You need to heal."

"And so do you. God protected us, Triese. He protected us and those with us. I am so sorry that it happened."

"It's not your fault, is it? Did you plant those bombs? And there were bombs that were found around the property." Triese frowned at the thought. "I don't understand, Teeg. I really don't. Where is God in all this? Couldn't He have prevented this?"

"He could have but He didn't. We don't know the reason why and may never understand it. All I know is that He protects us from danger most of the time. Sometimes, He allows something to happen that is in His plans for our lives. We can't stop that but He has His hand on our lives."

"I get that. I just don't have to like it." Triese sounded disgruntled at that.

"He is in control, Triese." Teeg turned his head as he heard footsteps. Toby had appeared, frowning at his brother. "Toby?"

"You're not supposed to be up yet, Teeg."

"No, that's what you think. The doctor said that I could be up and moving around, as long as I'm careful. And I will be. Now, we can leave, right?"

"We can. Where are you heading?"

"To Brit's, I think. So are you. And Triese needs to as well."

Triese's mouth opened and closed for a moment before she shrugged. Why not? At least that way she could keep an eye on Teeg.

Toby bit back a smile, not sure what had happened before he walked into the room. All he was aware of was that his brother was in danger as was his lady. And they had no idea why or who.

Teeg stared out of the truck window as Toby drove towards Brit's home. He could hear Triese muttering to herself but her voice was too low for him to understand her words.

Triese studied Teeg, a frown in place. She had no idea what was going on but she was sure that it involved her. Toby had been around to her hospital room and went over everything that had happened over the past couple of weeks. Triese had been puzzled as well. She had no enemies as far as she knew. Toby had asked if she could go over her photos as best she could and see if there was something there. She had agreed, staring at him with a look that said he had just asked a huge task of her.

Chapter 13

Three days later, Triese paced her home office. She was thinking about what Toby had asked her. Shaking her head, Triese sat at her desk, a pen in her hands. She thought through again what Toby had asked. There were just too many photos for her to go through them all. He would need to narrow the time frame before she would do that.

On her feet once more, Triese reached for her favourite camera and headed for her back yard. She locked the door behind her, her keys tucked into her jeans' pocket. She needed some photos of garden critters and today was the day that she chose to work on that.

Satisfied at last that she had what she needed, Triese sat back on her heels, her camera placed gently on the ground beside her. Her head bent as she began to pray and then just to wait in stillness and silence for her Father to speak to her and to quiet her heart. It was how she found the peace that she so desperately needed at times. It was an hour before she was on her feet, reaching for her camera, and then walking towards the house. She frowned at the man who sat on the steps.

"Teeg? What are you doing here? Aren't you supposed to be at home or something?" Triese sat beside him, her head tilted to watch him.

"I should be but I needed to be here with you. God sent me." Teeg had become used to following the nudges from God. For this lady, he would stand in front of her and protect her. He hadn't reasoned out yet that he loved her.

"He did? And did He tell you why?" Triese was almost angry at Teeg. He needed to rest and being here was not doing that.

"No, He did. Triese, what do you make of all of this?"

"Of all of this? I have no idea. I don't know who kidnapped me in the first place and destroyed my home. I have no idea who placed the bombs here and at your home. It's not making sense. I don't have any enemies that I know of."

"And neither do I. Someone wants to harm you. I don't want to see you hurt." Teeg was adamant that he had to protect her.

"And you can't protect me, Teeg. As much as you want to, you can't do God's work for Him. We can't be together all the time as much as you think we should be. We both have work that we need to do. We have activities that don't include each other." Triese smiled sadly at him. "You need to heal, Teeg."

"And so do you. I wish it had been different, Triese. I really do. I wish I could remember what happened and why we were out there looking that day."

"We were trying to figure out why I was dumped on that side of the creek. And then the storm hit. We never did find out why. And going back there again would answer that." She looked around. "Where's Andy?"

"He's with Brit. He was not happy with me when I left him there."

"He can come here any time. The yard is fenced so he wouldn't come to any harm." Triese rose and walked into the house, returning with bottles of water for each of them. "Here."

"Thank you." Teeg pointed at her camera. "What were you up to?"

"I needed pictures of garden critters." She reached for her camera and brought up the photos.

Teeg studied them, amazed at the talent that she showed.

"These are wonderful." He bit at his lip and then named a company. "You did their photos."

"I did but how did you know?"

Teeg shrugged. He couldn't say how he knew but he did.

"It has your stamp on them. You have a unique perspective on what you do." Teeg paused at the photo of a Painted Lady butterfly on a coneflower. "I like this one. It is so peaceful. We could use some of that peace right now."

Triese leaned against him to study the photo. She didn't think it was one of her better ones but she made a mental note to print it and frame it for Teeg. It was the least that she could do.

"We could, Teeg. I feel peace when I am out in nature. It is how I sometimes commune with my

Father. I always think of how we were prayed for in the garden."

Teeg nodded, his thoughts slipping away from the backyard for a moment.

"It's true, Triese. It is so true. We forget that, don't we? We forget that we have all of God's power and protection standing between us and danger. He is our Shield to life."

"That's true." She pointed behind her. "I have a shield in my house that was Dad's. He gave it to me years ago so that I would have a visual memory of it." She grew sober. "It was about the time when Tait disappeared. It was to go to Tait. Dad gave it to me. If and when Tait ever appears again, I will give it to him."

"Do you have any idea where he is?" Teeg studied the soberness and sadness on her face.

"Not a one. He was there one morning and by afternoon there was no sign of him. His phone was on his car seat and his car was parked in an area where he would never be found. The police found it two days after he disappeared. They couldn't tell us if he went on his own or if he was forcibly removed. Tait was a researcher of animals in the wild and how they have changed over the years. He was well known in that area even for his young age. He is only one year older than me. He graduated from university at age eighteen."

"That's young. And he would have been working ever since." Teeg made a mental note to speak with Toby and see what they could discover about Tait. “Have you tried to find him? I would hazard a guess that you have.”

“We have. We’ve hired private investigators. The detective in our home town is still looking but there are no leads. That’s what is so strange about it. He would not leave on his own and not tell us.” Triese reached to wipe away a tear, Teeg’s arm around her to hug her to him. “I miss him. I just want to know that he is alive and well and happy. I just don’t like it that we can’t find him.”

Teeg had to agree. He began to petition God to return Tait to his family. His lady was hurting and he wanted to take away that hurt.

Chapter 14

Toby paced around Teeg's cabin, listening to Ed as he described what had been found. He shook his head before he looked over at Teeg. Teeg stood on his back patio, his eyes following his brother. Toby knew that Teeg wanted to be out there and searching but he was well aware that he needed to wait.

"Do we have any idea why?" Toby's voice was quiet in the stillness of the early morning air.

"No, we don't. And that's frustrating. I know that you and Jason are looking into it but there are no answers. There was nothing on any of the bombs that would give any hint as to who manufactured them." Ed was frustrated at that.

"I see." Toby stared around, uncomfortable for a moment.

"You're nervous, Toby. Can't say that I blame you. Someone tried to take out either you or Teeg or even Triese. And that is something that needs to be solved and is being solved." Ed walked away at last.

Teeg stood beside Toby, his eyes searching around his home. He no longer felt safe there. And that dismayed him. This was his haven in life, a place where he could hide away from events and happenings. This was a place where he communed more deeply with his Heavenly Father. Now, he felt that the peace and safety were no longer present.

"Toby? Where do we stand with the investigation?" Teeg waited for his brother to react.

"Not where I would like to be. There is just no information to move forward. We can see evidence that both you and Triese are being watched and targeted. We just don't have the evidence we need to solve this. It's frustrating, Teeg. We want this over for you two." Toby turned his head slightly to watch his brother, seeing Triese walking rapidly towards them. He frowned. She wasn't supposed to be driving, not yet. How did she get here?

Teeg shrugged. It was about what he expected Toby to say. He turned as he heard a voice and found Triese running towards him. He simply opened his arms and swept her to his heart.

"Triese? What's wrong?" Teeg waited somewhat impatiently for her to speak.

"This!" Neither man had seen the envelope that she had clutched in her hand. "Who is doing this?"

Toby reached and gently removed the envelope from her hand. He stared at her for a moment, seeing the terror that was on her face. He could only imagine the drive out here. He removed the folded piece of paper and opened it. His face grew stern as he read it before he showed it to Teeg.

Teeg's anger flared as he read it. Who was going after his lady? That person was who he wanted. They just didn't know who it was. And they were threatening him as well.

"When did you get this?" Toby kept his voice measured as he re-read the letter. It was brutal, to say the least. Whoever it was that had precipitated this was not a very nice person, he decided. To threaten to kill

Triese and Teeg was about what he had expected. He had not expected it to be laid out in such a brutal manner.

Triese found safety as she described it as Teeg wrapped an arm tighter around her. She stared around, seeing the damage from the bomb but also knowing that God had been their shield that day and protected them from dying.

Toby walked away from his brother, studying the letter. He was frustrated and angry. There was nothing on the letter to indicate who was after Triese or who was threatening both Triese and Teeg. He reached for his phone, calling Tyler.

"Tyler? Triese just received a threatening letter. It threatens both Triese and Teeg. I'm with them now at Teeg's."

"Stay with them. I'm on my way. Is Roger on duty today?" Tyler was on his feet, heading for his car. He would have done that for anyone but when it was his nephew involved, it took a little bit more of his heart to deal with this.

"He is. I've sent a text off to him." Toby turned to watch his brother, seeing him watching himself in return. "I don't know where to turn, Tyler. I really don't. We don't have enough evidence to even begin to look at anyone."

"I know that you don't. You're doing the best that you can with the hand you've been dealt." Tyler's fingers tapped on his steering wheel as he waited for a red light to turn green. "Have you gone over everything that you can with Triese?"

"I have. So has Jason. There's just nothing there that we can see. Unless it comes back to her brother." Toby frowned at that thought. Was that where the answer lay?

"Her brother?" Tyler's foot hit the accelerator as he reached the edge of town and headed for his nephews.

"Her brother, Tait. He disappeared about two years ago. They have never been able to find him. Triese says that is not her brother. He would not just have walked away from his family." Toby drew in a deep breath. "And we need to try and find him, don't we?"

"We do. Have Jason contact the force in her town or whatever town it was he disappeared from. I would suspect that it is still an active case." Tyler slowed to turn into Teeg's driveway and parked before he walked in a rapid manner towards his nephews. He paused as he reached the cabin, watching his two nephews closely. He could see the stress and strain that they were dealing with.

Teeg turned as he heard a noise, fear growing in him. He sighed and his stance relaxed as he saw his uncle.

"Uncle Ty?" Teeg did not release Triese, who had crowded closer to him.

"Teeg? Triese? What have you gone and done now?" Tyler gave a grim smile, knowing that they were not at fault.

“What have we done? Nothing that I am aware of, Uncle Ty.” Teeg studied his home. The windows had been replaced and any damage had been repaired. But he still felt unsafe. The thing of it was that he didn’t want to leave his home but it might be necessary at some point.

“We know that, Teeg. Triese? We need to have a conversation about your brother. Toby and Jason need to be in on it.” Tyler’s gaze was compassionate as he spoke.

“I know. I wonder if this goes back to him. He just disappeared one day. We have had no word from him and we can’t find him. I want my brother.” Tears sparkled on her face as Teeg turned her into his shoulder, his arms tightening around her.

Chapter 15

Teeg moved through his cabin, seeing that any damage had been repaired. He was frustrated, however, with the headache that he was still suffering from. He needed to be working and didn't feel like it. Everyone had headed home, Toby taking Triese with her. She still didn't say how she had arrived. She just refused to say.

His hand reached to rest on Andy's head. Andy was edgy that day. Teeg could not blame him. He still felt that way. He had no idea why.

Andy paced the house, his nose sniffing around. There was something off in the house and he wanted to find it. He nosed into the clothes cupboard and then went running for Teeg. Andy caught at Teeg's hand and tugged him with him.

Teeg stared down at Andy and then at the cupboard. He reached for a flashlight and then began a systemic search of the cupboard. He pulled out the device that had been planted there and frowned at it. He walked back into the kitchen and dropped it onto the table. He had no idea what it was.

"Toby? I just found something in my closet." Teeg had reached out to his brother.

"What is it?" Toby's hand was already turning the steering wheel of his car to head back towards Teeg's cabin.

"I have no idea. Andy searched the house, sensing something was off. He dragged me to the cupboard." Teeg pulled out a chair and sank into it. He was exhausted and didn't need this. His plans for the day had already flown out of the window. This just added to it.

Toby parked near the cabin, hesitating for a moment before he reached for his car door. He was worried beyond what he had ever been. This shouldn't be happening to Teeg. Toby frowned at the front door before he tapped and then walked in.

Teeg looked up from where he was still sitting. He didn't say a word. Andy had rushed at Toby and grabbed at his pant leg, pulling him forward. Toby stared down at the dog, knowing that Andy was worried and that for Andy to be that worried meant something was definitely wrong. Both brothers had learned to trust Andy in a way that most people would not trust a dog.

"Andy, what's wrong? What did you find, boy?" Toby dropped down into a seat near his brother, his eyes on him. "Teeg?"

"I don't know any more, Toby. I really don't. This used to be my sanctuary, but it doesn't feel like that any more. This has me doubting my faith even though I know that God is in control."

"He is, Teeg. That He is. It is very tough to trust sometimes, especially when you're going through something dark. That's when He's our light and lamp. He walks through this with us, always has. There are many times over the years that I have doubted and have had to walk away for a few moments just to get my perspective back. It's hard at times. But I hear what you aren't saying."

Teeg nodded. He and his brother had spoken many times about this. Why was he going through this? He had no idea. His thoughts turned to prayer and that prayer included his lady as he was now beginning to think of Triese.

"I have no idea what that is." Teeg pointed to the device. "Do you know?"

Toby looked at it closely before he reached for it. He sighed. It was motion-activated, he decided, and designed to record conversation. His finger went to his lips as Teeg opened his mouth to speak. Toby was on his feet, heading outside, the device turned off and then dropped into an evidence bag.

Teeg had followed his brother outside. He was frowning, he knew, not knowing what was going on.

"Toby? What is that?"

"A recording device of some kind." Toby looked contrite even as he heard the sounds of nature in his ears. "We never searched your home, Teeg. We should have." He walked away, heading into the cabin and beginning a systemic search. He was not shocked to find other devices hidden away.

Teeg stood in the doorway, his eyes on his brother, astounded at the number of devices that Toby was finding. He stepped away, his emotions overcoming him for a moment. Anger was uppermost. He wanted whoever it was that had done this and wanted them right that moment.

Tyler had approached as Toby walked away. His steps paused as he watched his nephew before he walked into the cabin. Toby turned as his uncle appeared.

"Toby? What are you finding?"

Toby looked around, a tight look on his face.

"Those." He pointed to the evidence bags on the table. "Someone was through Teeg's home and planted those. I wonder if that was when the bomb went off. It would be so easy for them to sneak in when we were unconscious."

"That is likely the case. What about Teeg's security system?"

"It's been damaged. We would not have known that. Teeg hasn't been around or aware that much to have picked up on that. It was working before this and he would have had no question that it still would have been working." Toby pointed to the security panel. "I checked it. It was tampered with."

Tyler felt himself growing even angrier. This should not have been happening. He walked away, outside to find Teeg. Teeg had slumped in a deck chair, his hand resting on Andy's head. Andy's chin was on Teeg's thigh, a soft whine coming from the dog.

Sitting near his nephew, Tyler remained quiet, praying instead for Teeg and then Triese. He also prayed for Toby and Brit, knowing how they were impacted by this.

"Uncle Ty? Who did this?"

“We don’t know, Teeg. I wish that I could tell you that we did. We just don’t have the information that we need to solve this.” Tyler was contrite as he spoke. He wanted this over for his nephew. His gaze turned to the forest around them, knowing that there could be someone hid there and they would never know.

“I know, Uncle Ty. I want this over. I am tired of living like this. I worry about my family. I also worry about Triese. I don’t want to see her hurt. This isn’t making any sense.” Teeg drew in a deep breath. “Toby said that he was looking into her brother.”

“He is. It’s something that needs to be done. We need to find him. That may solve what you two are going through. Triese is most at risk. You are at risk just because of your friendship with her. Whoever this is has connected you two and has gone after you to get to her.” Tyler’s hand went up as Teeg’s mouth opened. “Hear me out, son. You rescued her. She is important to you. Anyone knows that you don’t date but you are moving in that direction with Triese. They know that and will keep after you. We can’t protect you two, not without having more information as to why.”

Chapter 16

Triese tramped as quietly as she could along a stream bank just outside of town. She was on a search for some new photos that she needed and didn't know where to find them. Her mind was not really on her search. Instead, her thoughts were on Teeg. It was mid-week and she had not seen him. In fact, she had not heard from him at all. Triese would not reach out to him. That wasn't her place, she decided.

A sound beside her stopped her in her tracks. She froze for a moment before looking that way. She drew in her breath, her camera raised. A doe and its fawn stood there, silently watching Triese for any sign of danger. Triese snapped the photos that she could before she silently walked on, turning to watch as the doe and her fawn approached the stream. Triese's mind tracked to the verse in Psalms that spoke of a deer looking for water. She raised her eyes to the sky, thanking God for His reminder of that. She needed that reminder.

Late that afternoon, Triese set her camera on her office desk and turned. She felt grubby and wanted to clean up before she found something to eat. Reaching for her phone as she prepared a meal, a soft smile crossing her face. Teeg had been in touch. He was heading her way with a meal. Was she home? Her fingers flew across the phone key board as she answered.

Teeg stood in the entryway of Triese's home, thankful that she was there and fine. He set the food bag down and opened his arms, Triese almost running into his hug. He held on to her, a prayer whispering out, the words of which he never heard himself. A kiss was dropped on the top of her head before Triese moved back and stared up at him, a question on her face.

"Triese? Did you have a good day?" Teeg reached for the bag of food and headed for her kitchen.

"I did. I spent time out in nature. I need to show you some of the photos." She spun, intent on heading for her camera before Teeg wrapped an arm around her. "Teeg?"

"We'll eat first, darling. And then we pray. And then, you'll show me all the wonderful photos that you took today." Teeg studied her for a moment. "You know, I need you to come with me see days and take photos. I see so much out there in God's wilderness." Teeg didn't look at her, intent on taking out their burgers and fries.

"You do? Okay, I guess. I can do that." Triese reached for bottles of water for them. "Do you want to eat inside or outside?"

Teeg looked down at the food and then at her. He was drawn to her once more not just because of her physical beauty. He loved the spirit and strength that was her.

"Inside, I think. The clouds are moving in and it's getting slightly chilly." He drew back her chair so that she could sit. He then sat with a hand reaching for hers. His head bowed as he asked a blessing on their food, his voice pausing before he continued and asked for God to be their Shield and Protector over the next few weeks. Teeg was deeply worried about Triese without knowing exactly why.

Triese raised her head at last, feeling as if God had been right there. She felt a sense of peace that she had not felt for a few days. Teeg was the reason why. She was puzzled at that. Triese was just not aware that she was falling in love with the tall, handsome man sharing a meal with her and that he was wiggling his way into her heart.

Their meal over, Triese retrieved her camera and sat once more at the table. She listened to Teeg as he whistled softly. He was making coffee for them. Her head tilted and a soft smile crossed her face. Without knowing, he had chosen the chorus about the deer and water.

"Teeg? That chorus that you're whistling? I thought of those verses today." She handed over her camera. "This is why."

Teeg set their mugs of coffee on the table and then sat, reaching for her camera. He smiled at her as he did so, not realizing that it was a smile that he used only for her. His eyes dropped to the camera and he drew in a soft, deep breath.

"These are beautiful. I feel as if I'm right there looking at them in real life. You have a rare talent, Triese, an ability to look right into God's creation and pull out the best." He dropped a kiss on her cheek without thinking. His attention went back to the photos as he moved through them. His hand paused at the next to last one, his eyes on the man hidden behind a tree and just barely visible. “Triese? Did you notice this?”

Triese stared at him before tilting his hand to study the photo. Horror covered her face.

“I never saw him. He was following me?”

“It’s possible. Can we download these and then send this one to Toby? He’ll work with Roger to figure out who the man is.” Teeg was on his feet, following Triese as she almost ran for her office and connected her camera to the computer.

Once the photos were downloaded, Triese moved aside so that Teeg could send the email to his brother. Toby was quick to respond, just to say that he had the photo and would work on it. Could the two of them just stay safe, he asked?

Teeg gave a tight smile at that before he was on his feet and hugging his lady. He didn’t want any harm to come to her but he did need to be on the move. He had an early day the next day, having to travel out of town for a conference.

“I’m away tomorrow, Triese. Will you be all right?”

Triese frowned at him.

“You need to live your life, Teeg. As much as you want to protect me, you can’t be with me all the time. And no, we are not getting married. We aren’t anywhere close to that, if we will ever be.”

“I know, Triese. I do want to date you. I have never asked that of a lady before. You are important to me.” Teeg was on the move towards the front door.

"Come and lock up after me. Toby said that he's going to find you tomorrow. He doesn't know if your house was searched after it was damaged."

Triese sighed. She didn't need Toby coming around on the next day. She had work to do and deadlines to meet.

"It was and nothing was found. My security system has not been breached, if that's a concern." Triese locked up after him and then returned to her office. She stared at her computer before she walked away from it. She was not ready to work on anything that night. Instead, Triese headed for her bed and her Bible. She needed some God time and some time spent in silence before Him.

Chapter 17

A week later, Triese walked through the downtown area, not sure why she was there but she had felt compelled to be there. She searched the faces of those who passed her. Triese had to admit to herself that she was really missing Tait that day. Her parents had been in touch, just asking if she was okay. They promised to come soon but work had restricted where they could move at present. That dismayed all of them.

Triese's feet slowed as she approached an alley. She was not comfortable walking by it as her feet stopped. She was afraid and didn't know why. Her eyes raised to the entrance of the alley and her hands covered her mouth. Triese stared at the unkempt man who stood there, his clothes ragged and dirty.

"Tait? Tait?" Triese didn't know if she was seeing things or not. That man resembled her brother.

The man shoved himself away from the brick wall of the building and stumbled slightly as he walked towards her. As he grew closer, certainty grew within Triese that it was indeed her brother.

Tait Cameron stopped just short of his sister. It had been over two years since he had seen her, two long hard years that had taken their toll on him. He reached out a hand that was shaking before Triese moved in on him and hugged him. His arms went around her in a tight hug as both brother and sister sobbed.

Triese stepped back from him, her hands on his forearms.

“Tait? Where have you been?” Triese looked around before she linked an arm with her brother’s arm and led him to her car. She shoved him inside to a seat in the front. She headed for her home and then stopped at a store.

Triese ran inside the store and was back in short order, dropping the bags onto the back seat. She drove rapidly for her home, opening the garage door and heading into it. She was out of the car, the bags in her hand, before she was pulling Tait from the car. Triese shoved him inside and handed him the bags.

“You need to shower and shave, Tait. Go and do that. I’ll find something easy for you to eat. We’ll talk, I promise. I want to know where you have been and what has happened to you. I just thank God that you are here.” Triese stared at her brother, seeing the changes that were evident.

“Thanks, Triese. I do need to talk to you. I also need to find a police officer to speak with. I didn’t leave on my own.” Tait swayed for a moment, the rough treatment that he had undergone wreaking havoc in his body. He turned and trudged away, heading for the bathroom and a long hot shower.

Triese stared after him and then headed for the kitchen. She had soup in the freezer that she pulled out and put on the stove to heat. A package of crackers was opened and set on the table. Coffee was put on to drip. She paced with her arms wrapped around herself.

Her thoughts were troubled. She had no idea where Tait had been but he was here now.

Reaching for her phone, Triese's fingers hesitated before she sent a text off to Toby, just asking if he could stop by her place in the next hour. Something had come up that she needed to speak with him about. Her next text message went off to Teeg. Could he come to her home? She needed him. She had good news but there was something that made her afraid.

Teeg stared at the text message, his thoughts troubled and his heart dropping as he read it. Something had happened and he was an hour from his cabin. He shouldered his backpack and whistled for Andy. As soon as he reached his truck, the pack was dropped into the back seat as Andy leapt into the cab and over to the passenger's seat. Driving almost too fast, Teeg headed for his lady, stopping in front of her home. He frowned as he recognized Toby's police cruiser. That was not what he had expected.

Tapping at the front door, Teeg walked into the home and found Triese waiting for him. She simply walked up to him and into his hug, sobs shaking her body. Teeg frowned. This was not what he had expected to find. His prayer whispered in her ear but this time, it did not soothe her.

"Triese, darling? What's going on?" Teeg kept his voice low, trying to understand the words of the men who he could hear speaking in the kitchen.

"It's Tait. He was waiting for me downtown. I don't know why I went there but I did. God must have sent me. He was waiting for me. I brought him here. Toby's speaking with him. I don't know where he was or what happened. He needs to talk with Toby and then I need to find someone to look him over."

"I know of someone, a friend who will come here." Teeg moved her to the living room and to a seat on the couch. He sat beside her, an arm around her. "Talk to me, Triese. Tell me what happened."

Triese was silent. She had no words to say or even didn't know what to say. Teeg just waited for her to speak, holding her and praying for her. Triese was waiting for Toby and Tait to appear. She knew that it would take time. Tait had over two years to explain. She sighed as her phone chimed, taking it as Teeg handed it to her. It was her parents.

Hesitating, Triese sent her parents a message, simply stating that Tait was with her and could they come? She had no idea the consternation that this message started with her parents who immediately began to make plans to join their son and daughter. A message was sent to Triese simply stating that they were on their way.

Teeg watched the emotions flickering across her face. He didn't need to say anything or ask anything. He could wait. For now, he would simply pray for her and for her family. His feeling was that Tait's reappearance was deliberate and meant to harm his lady. He would do what he could to alleviate that fear.

On his feet, Teeg walked to the front door, opening it to find Tyler and a physician friend, Rex, standing there. Toby had asked his uncle to find a physician and bring that person to Triese's home. Tait was there and needed that assessment.

Tyler studied his nephew before he looked past him at Triese. It was a very emotional moment for Triese and he was worried about her. He headed for the kitchen with Rex in tow, leaving Teeg to head back for his lady.

"Uncle Ty has brought in a physician, darling. Rex will look Tait over and then make any recommendations that he needs to. We'll keep him as safe as we can."

Chapter 18

Triese watched the doorway, wanting to talk with her brother and demand answers as to where she was but knowing that she had to wait until Toby was done with him. She had no idea how long that would take. Triese settled back against Teeg, not realizing that he still had her in his arms.

"Triese? Talk to me." Teeg broke the silence between them at last. The only sound in the room, other than the faint sounds of conversation from the kitchen, had been the tick of the mantle clock.

"What can I say, Teeg?" She twisted slightly to look up at him. "You're holding on to me!"

"I am. You need to be held right now. Your emotions are in a whirlwind. You want to talk to your brother and right now you can't. You want your parents and they're not here. You're struggling to trust and believe in a situation you have never been in before. This is when you have to trust and that's hard. It's hard to trust in Someone you can't see."

"It is hard, Teeg. It is so hard. And I need to be working. I have photos that I need to finish off today."

Teeg was on his feet, his hand tugging at hers to draw her to her feet. Hand in hand, he walked her to her office and shoved her into her chair.

"Work away, darling. I'll sit here and watch what you're doing. I find it fascinating." Teeg was soon immersed in watching what she was doing. His head turned an hour later as he heard footsteps heading their way and then stopping at the doorway to the office.

Toby watched his brother for a moment before his attention turned to Triese. He did need to speak with her. At the moment, Tait was closed into a bedroom with Rex being assessed. He looked rough, Toby decided, not surprising from what he had gone through. God had protected him. Toby just wasn't sure how he managed to get away or if he had been allowed to leave. The latter was likely the case.

Triese roused from her work, satisfied that she had done the best that she could. Her proofs were sent off to her client before she sat back, searching for Teeg. Teeg's hand went out for hers and she clutched at him as if she was clutching a lifeline. Her eyes then spied Toby in the doorway.

"Toby?" Triese was on her feet, Teeg with her, her hand still in his.

"Triese? Rex is looking your brother over. Tyler is preparing a meal for us. I know that Tait has eaten but he'll join us for coffee once Rex has done what he needs to. Tait may need to be seen at the hospital for imaging. Rex will pull bloodwork to send it. Come and sit with us. I need to speak with you prior to your brother telling you what he can. Some of what he went through has to remain quiet until the investigation is complete. And it does involve you."

"I thought that it would." Triese sighed before she leaned against Teeg.

"It does. We'll figure it out. Some of what he said ties in with hat you just went through. Some of it does not." Toby waited patiently for Triese to move. When she didn't, he looked at Teeg who simply shrugged. They would wait for Triese to move. They had to.

Triese shook her head at last and then moved away from the brothers. She headed for the kitchen and then past Tyler to the backyard. She sank onto the steps of the deck, her chin on her hands, elbows planted on her knees. She just waited but what she was waiting for? She wasn't sure.

The closing of the back door startled her and then she felt someone sitting beside her. She could tell the person was hesitant to do that before an arm wrapped around her. Triese leaned against her brother before sobs shook her body. Tait was in tears as well, not sure what to say to his sister. The siblings just sat there, watching as the sun sank towards the horizon. It had been years since they had been together. They felt like strangers but were drawn closer for some reason.

"Tait? What happened to you?" Triese's voice was barely audible.

"I don't know how to start, Triese. I tried to get away and to find you. You have been threatened by the ones who held me. I just couldn't get away. Not until last night. Someone walked in to where I was being held and walked out with me. I could see the men holding me there but they didn't look at us as we walked by them. I think God sent an angel. He brought me here even though I protested that this is not where you were. He left me down town where you found me. I can't explain it."

"God did that, Tait. We both know that we believe that. Your faith has been shaken and tossed around but you still believe."

"I do, Triese. I do. I don't know that I should, given what I went through but I do believe. I never lost that. Many times the only thing I could do was pray and try and remember the verses that we memorized."

"And we memorized a lot. Dad saw to that." Her head rubbed against his shoulder for a moment. This was her brother beside her. She knew him. Yet, she didn't. Not any more. He had changed because of what he had gone through.

"He did. How are Mom and Dad?" Tait was afraid to ask, afraid that they were dead and he would never see them again.

"They have been looking for you and grieving for you as well. They're on their way. I sent a text to them when you were speaking with Toby. Wait until they are here to tell me your story. That way, you only have to tell it once. We'll work through it. The spare room where Rex examined you is yours to use."

"Thanks, sis." Tait bit at his lip for a moment. "This Teeg? Who is he?"

"Teeg? He's a close friend. We have shared an adventure together that I'll tell you about. He's also brother to Toby and nephew to Tyler. They've been a real support to me over the last couple of weeks."

"That's what Toby said. He didn't elaborate on what had been going on but he did state that you are in danger. And that I am likely part of it." Tait had begun to worry about his sister.

"I am, Tait. And I do think that you are part of it." Triese swiped at the tears on her cheeks. "I worried so much about you. I thought that you were dead but I never felt grief for that. I felt the grief of not having you around."

"And I grieved too, Triese. We'll talk and I'll talk with Teeg. When Mom and Dad get here, we'll talk. Toby wants to be there and I'm sure that Teeg would be there."

"He will be there. We'll make sure of that." Triese rose at last, finding Tait standing as well. "I need to eat, Tait, but you've already eaten."

"I have but the coffee is great. I have not enjoyed a cup of coffee in a long time." Tait hugged his sister, holding on a lot longer than usual, before he turned them to the door. The twilight was dropping behind them. Neither one of them saw the man standing nearby watching them, on guard for any harm that might come to them.

Teeg reached to hug Triese before he reached to hug Tait. That surprised the other man but not the others in the room. There was silence in the room as well, each one absorbed in their own thoughts.

Chapter 19

The next afternoon, Triese was on her feet, walking away from the photos that she had been working on. She needed a break and she also needed to find her brother. Not seeing him in the house, she headed for the back door and opened it. A smile lit her face. Tait was seated near the back of the yard, Andy almost in his lap. Teeg sat nearby before he was on his feet and heading for her. He hugged Triese before looking down at her.

"Having a good day, darling?" Teeg grinned down at her as she frowned up at him.

"I don't know. I've spent it working on my photos. You're here?"

"I am. Andy wanted to come and find you. I couldn't say no to him." Teeg laughed as she shook a finger at her. "He's worried about your brother."

"He is, isn't he? Does he always do that when he's worried?" Triese looked around Teeg to watch Tait and Andy. "Tait has always had a way with dogs."

"Try to comfort someone? He does. He's sensitive that way. He picks up on things and emotions that we don't. I usually don't let him go as far as he is with Tait, but Tait allowed it. He needs that comfort." Teeg turned her to walk towards her brother. "When do your parents arrive?"

Triese reached to turn his wrist to look at the time on his watch.

"Their plane would have landed about an hour ago. By the time that they get their luggage and then a car, it would have been thirty minutes or more." She felt Teeg shift slightly. "Teeg?"

"Toby spoke with them. He's picking them up so they don't have to look for a car. The officer from your town put him in touch with them."

"Thank you. That helps. It will make it easier for them. They don't have to worry and then try and drive as well. I worried about that. It is so easy to be distracted when you're worrying about something. And before you say it, I know. We do God's work when we worry. But it's part of our humanness that we do. We can't help it, you know." Triese reached to greet Andy who had run towards her and then stood up to sniff at her face before his tongue was out to swipe across her cheek. She hugged him and then watched as he ran back to Andy and with one leap was on his knee. Her face lit up with her laughter. "Did he really just do that?"

"He did. And it is what he does if he can get away with it." Teeg's laughter rang through the yard. He turned slightly as he heard a sound, frowning at his brother. His eyes then took in the couple with him. "Triese, darling. You need to turn around."

"Why? I need to talk with Tait." She frowned at him and tried to move forward only to find Teeg's arm preventing that. "Teeg? What are you doing?"

"Turn around, darling. Toby's here." Teeg was watching her intently and saw the moment when it sank in that Toby was there and that if Toby was there, her parents would be as well.

Triese spun quickly, only kept on her feet by Teeg's arm around her. Her eyes sought Toby's who nodded at her, a smile on his face. Her gaze moved to the side and then her face lit up. She struggled to escape Teeg's arm and then ran towards her parents, scooped into a tight hug by them both. Tait had looked up and then risen to his feet, hesitantly walking towards the trio.

Timothy looked up at that point, an almost inaudible sound coming from him before he was across the yard with his son in his arms. Both men's bodies shook from the intensity of their emotions even as tears streamed down their cheeks. Timothy felt a hand on his back and moved back to let Abygayle to move in on her son. Abygayle hugged her son, praising God that her son was there with them once more.

Emotions were high as they all found seats in the backyard. Tait was between his parents who would not let him out of their sight. Triese was seated nearby, Andy tight to her. The dog could sense her heightened emotions and was trying his best to bring comfort to her. Teeg paused as he walked back towards the four, a frown on his face. He could sense the danger drawing closer to them and that scared him. All he could do was pray for them.

Toby paused beside his brother, a tray holding a plate of sandwiches and also fruit held in his hands. Teeg was holding a tray of mugs of coffee.

"This is hurting them all, Teeg." Toby had not said what Tait had told him. He couldn't but he had asked Tait to speak with his family. Tait had been hesitant to but knew that he had to.

"I know. There's not a lot that we can do about what he went through. That's in the past. But we need to watch Triese carefully for now. And we need to watch you as well. They'll go after you to get to her." Toby waited for his words to sink into Teeg's thoughts.

Teeg froze at Toby's words, his gaze shifting from Triese to his brother and then to Tait. He had thought that but to have Toby utter those words had just confirmed his worst thoughts.

"I get that, Toby. I just don't see how we can avoid everyone and every event." Triese shifted on his feet, careful not to juggle the tray and slop coffee out of the cups.

"It will be difficult. You're out there in the wilderness doing what you need to. You can't have anyone with you. The same goes for Triese. She's out and about taking her photos and then spending time here working on them." Toby was frustrated but trying not to show it.

Triese was on her feet and headed for the men, a frown on her face.

"Guys? What's going on?" She planted herself in front of them.

"Just talking, darling." Teeg leaned forward and dropped a kiss on her cheek, a move that highly surprised her.

"Well, what did you decide for me to do that I'm not willing to do?" Triese frowned even harder as the brothers began to laugh.

"Nothing, Triese. Not one thing." Toby walked on by her, setting the tray down on a small table that was waiting for it. He sat, his eyes closing for a moment as he prayed.

Timothy watched his daughter closely as she stood talking with Teeg. He saw the look on Teeg's face and nodded. His daughter had found the knight that had been wrapped in her bedtime stories as a child. He liked what he knew of Teeg from Toby. Toby had been open with them, talking about his family. He looked over at Abygayle who was nodding at him. She had seen the same thing that he had.

Triese raised her head ninty minutes later. She was not happy with what was going on at all. She felt at a loss, unable to move forward and yet knowing that she had to. She felt the nudge from God that she had expected come and she felt a sense of peace move through her. God loved her and wanted only the best for her. That was a given. It was also a given that He was her Shield and Protector and to stand in His place, He had sent Teeg into her life. And Teeg had become a big part of her life. She finally had acknowledged to herself that she was falling in love with the tall, handsome man who was trying so hard to protect her and shield her from danger.

Chapter 20

Teeg was on his feet and heading for the house. He carried the trays that were empty. Tait moved with him, finding it more comfortable to be on his feet and walking around. He enjoyed the freedom that he had not had for two years.

"Teeg? Are your parents coming?" Tait watched the fresh pot of coffee as it dripped through its cycle.

"They are." Teeg glanced at the clock. "They should be here by now." He turned as he heard a tap at the door and headed that way to find his parents and Brit waiting for him. He hugged his mother and sister and then silently pointed towards the backyard. They walked that way, waiting for Teeg and Tait to join them.

Timothy was on his feet, reaching to shake Teeg's parents' hands and then hugging Brit. Once they had sorted out their seats, Timothy simply bowed his head and prayed. He knew that God was in the midst of them and that by praying as he had was simply acknowledging that fact.

Tait looked around as they raised their heads again. He frowned at he was that Tyler had joined them. Tyler shook his head at him, indicating that he was there as family only and not as an officer. His glance went to Toby who also shook his head. Today, it was about family and not anything else. Today was the day that the healing needed for the family would begin.

“Tait? This is going to be had for us to hear but even harder for you to speak about.” Tyler took the lead in talking. He felt that God wanted him to. “If at any time you need to take a break, do so. We have the rest of the day and into tomorrow if you need to take that time. You are a victim of crime and will need to find someone to counsel you. That we will work on with you. For now, we are here as family only. Toby will make notes if he needs to but that will not affect how you talk or what you say. Just start talking. If we have questions, we will ask when you are done unless we need to clarify something as you are speaking.”

Tait nodded, his emotions raw on his face. He didn't want to talk. He felt ashamed that he had been kidnapped and kept that way for two years. He had tried many times to escape only to be thwarted. Tait realized that he had not been that far away from Red Oak and his sister. He frowned at the thought before his brow cleared. That was done deliberately, he decided.

“I don't know quite where to start.” Tait blinked rapidly. “I guess I have to go back to before I was kidnapped. I had felt that I had been followed for a couple of weeks but when I looked around me, I didn't see anyone who stood out. I guess that I just didn't see them.” Tait paused his words, his eyes on Triese. “I'm sorry, Triese. The men who took me? They were friends of ours or who we thought were friends.” He named the men, causing Triese to pale. “I know that you stopped any contact with them about a month before this all happened. I still don't understand why I was taken.”

Tait thought back to what had happened. He still couldn't understand it. It was not making a lot of sense. He had been asked for nothing and not to do anything. He had just been kept locked up.

Tait had been at home that day, just puttering around his apartment. He was looking forward to a night out with friends when the doorbell to his apartment had sounded. Tait had frowned, not expecting anyone at his door. Opening it, his hands had raised as he stared at the gun pointed at his chest. Tait had recognized the man as a so-called friend.

"Walt? What are you doing?" Tait's voice had been tight.

"You're coming with us, Tait. And that means now." Walt shoved towards Tait, making him move backward. The sudden push on his chest caused Tait to stumble and fall. He was dragged to his feet and then dragged from his apartment. His calls for help were silenced as a gag was tightened over his mouth. Handcuffs clicked around his wrists as he was shoved into a van with darkened windows and then onto the floor. He felt his feet tied tightly with a coarse rope. His head went down on the carpeted floor of the van as he prayed for safety and a way to escape.

A short ride later, Tait's feet were released and he was dragged roughly across the carpet, leaving rug burns on his face and arm. Pulled from the van, he was hurried into a house and then to a room in the centre of the home. The handcuffs were removed but the gag was left in place. Tait ran for the door as it closed but was unable to escape. His hand slapped at the closed door as his head went down against it. A few moments let him gather his breath. Tait turned to study the room. It was sparse in furnishing, just a chair and a bed. He walked over to a door and found a washroom. He was puzzled at what had happened. Tait thought that Walt was a friend, but what friend did this? Had he been involved in crime all along and now Tait had become part of it? He worried about his sister and his parents. He had had no chance to let them know that he had disappeared.

Late that afternoon, the door opened and Walt appeared with a tray that he dropped onto the small table near the bed. He sneered at Tait who just stood and watched him. Walt walked away, the man standing in the door moving backwards out of his way before the door was shut and locked.

Days turned into weeks. Tait was allowed out of the room for a few hours at a time but was kept under close guard. He had taken a chance a few times to run for the door and out of it but had always been tackled and then returned to the room. He would not be allowed out for days after any attempt.

Tait was puzzled. He was asked for nothing and told nothing. He was not forced to do anything. This didn't make sense. If it was a true kidnapping, he would have been forced to be part of a ransom demand.

Growing weary of being locked into one room, Tait asked for a Bible. He needed it. Walt had not given it to him for weeks after he had asked but finally handed him one. Tait just took it in silence and then turned away, finding a seat in the chair. He didn't see Walt staring at him in puzzlement and then anger before the door was slammed shut after him.

Tait lost track of the days that he was held captive. He knew that it was months but didn't realize that the months had added up to two years. He had tried to keep optimistic but that was difficult. His only companion was his Bible and his Heavenly Father.

One day, Tait touched the door, surprised to find it sliding open. He hesitated, sure that it was a trap. He peeked out and searched for one of his kidnappers. He didn't see anyone. Walking quietly and carefully to the back door, he looked for anyone who would stop him. There was no one. He opened the door and then snuck down the steps and towards the street.

Tait paused as he saw an older man waiting for him. He didn't walk forward, instead letting the man approach him.

"Tait? You don't know me but I've been watching out for you. The men who kidnapped you are delayed elsewhere for now. Come with me." The man pointed behind him. "I have a truck here. I'll get you to your family. I understand that your sister is in Red Oak. That's only twenty minutes from here."

Tait was apprehensive but he also felt a sense of trust for the man. That was unusual for him, given that he had been away from people for a couple of years as he found out later. The man drove rapidly away from that town towards Red Oak, heading for his own place. Tait was given clean clothes and then a place to eat and sleep.

The man stood over Tait as he slept before his eyes turned upwards.

“I found him, Lord, and got him to safety. I’ve done what You’ve asked. Now, I need to get him back with his family and then watch out for them. I know what You’ve asked of me.” He walked away, heading for the door and the outdoors. He walked towards Triese’s home, intent on finding a way to send her to the down town area the next morning.

Chapter 21

Tait had been awoken the next morning by a shake to his shoulder. He had frozen for a moment before he heard the voice of the man who had rescued him. He sat on the side of the bed, feeling relief that he was free from being held captive. Tait didn't know the man but he trusted him.

It was early morning when the man had led Tait from his home and to the down town area. He had silently pointed to an alleyway, positioning Tait there. He simply told him to wait there. Someone would be along shortly who would recognize him. The man had disappeared before Tait could say anything.

Tait had slumped against the brick wall of the building, intently watching for whoever it was. He had drawn in a deep breath as the lady walked towards him and then her steps had slowed. He shoved away from the brick wall and headed towards her, hugging her to himself as she threw herself at him. Tait felt a hand on his back keeping him upright but he knew that no one was behind him. He looked up with a thanks to God for that.

Overcome with emotions, Tait had simply hugged his sister. It had been two long years since he had seen her and he could not understand how she was there. He had simply nodded and gone with her, asking no questions. He had taken the bedroom that Triese had pointed him to, stretching out to sleep once more. The release of stress had caused him to want to sleep. He didn't know that Triese had reached out to their parents who had been shocked that Tait was there but had promised to be there as soon as they could.

Tait came back to the present day, his head bowed in shame. His mother's arms were around him as she wept. He could feel his father's arms around them both and heard his father's prayer for him.

Triese was overcome with tears. She had not realized that this had been so bad for her brother. None of them had expected to ever see him again. That he was here was a promise God had kept. They just had to figure out how what he went through affected Triese. She turned her head into Teeg's shoulder, finding his arms tight around her.

Toby and Tyler shared a look. There was more to the story than Tait had said. He had been open and honest with Toby the day before. He had agreed that certain details needed to be kept quiet and he would work with Toby over the coming days to try and find his kidnappers. Triese had been threatened but they had no idea why.

Titus was on his feet as was Sari. They collected the empty mugs and headed for the house. Fresh coffee was prepared by Sari as Titus found the food that Triese had bought for Andy. He smiled. Andy had Triese wrapped around his paw, Titus could tell, as he spied the water bowl and food bowl that were neatly placed on a mat near the back door. Andy had worked his way into Triese's life and Titus was not surprised. He dropped the food into the bowl and watched as the dog headed for it.

"What can we do, Titus, to help?" Sari's hand rested on the countertop for a moment.

"I don't know, sweetheart. We'll find out what we can do. We have friends who we can reach out to who will be willing to help." Titus reached to hug his wife, knowing that she was upset for Triese.

"That we do. Richard would be a good one to speak with." Sari spoke of a friend from a nearby town who had a security team.

"I talked with him last night, sweetheart. We'll ask Tait if he wants to speak with him." Titus reached to hug his wife before he picked up the tray with their mugs of coffee. "How many times have we served coffee to friends in need?"

"Too many to count, Titus. Far too many to count." Sari watched her sons and her daughter, seeing that they were trying hard to cover up their emotions and not succeeding very well.

Triese was on her feet, heading for her family to join in the group hug. Her sobs shook her body without her knowing the true reason why. She knew that she was terrified and not just for herself. She was terrified for Teeg as well. Somehow, someone had connected the two of them and they had to find out why.

Teeg rose and walked away. He had to. His emotions were too high at the moment for him to stay seated. Brit was on her feet, walking over to Teeg and wrapping an arm around his. They paced together, neither saying a word. They didn't need to.

Triese rose at last, looking for Teeg who was standing nearby waiting for her. She ran to him, his arms closing around her. Tyler and Toby had walked away, heading for the front of the house to have a deep conversation. They were puzzled as well as to why Tait had been kidnapped. Nothing he had said explained it.

Tait was exhausted and excused himself to head for the bedroom he was using. He stretched out, tears on his face. He didn't hear his father follow him and then reach for a blanket to cover his son as he had when Tait was young. He was distressed at what Tait had said and wanted more answers, more answers that were not forthcoming.

Triese walked her yard late that night. Her parents had retired for the night. Tait had not been up since he had stretched out that afternoon. She was troubled, more troubled than she had been. She had not expected to hear that Walt had been involved. Triese had never trusted him and had always felt a sense of evil around him. All she could do was praise God for His protection of her brother. Her phone vibrating stopped her in her tracks, a hand coming to her chest.

Pulling out her phone, a smile crossed her face. Teeg had sent a text message, just saying that he was praying for her and that he loved her. Triese was surprised at that before her face softened. Her fingers flew over the keyboard as she responded to him.

Triese did not see the man who was standing near the back of the yard. He was the man who had rescued Tait. His duties were not done, he knew. He had to watch out for both Triese and Tait. He had no choice in the matter. It was what God had asked of him and he would not say no to God.

Triese headed for the house, her steps slowing for a moment before she ran for the house and shut and locked the door behind her. The security system was set before Triese headed for her office. She had work to do and that had to be done that night. She sighed. She was exhausted to the bone, Triese decided, but her commitment to her clients came before her own sleep. The men pacing around the house saw the office light on well into the morning but they had no way to enter the house. Her security system was too good.

Tait shot up on his bed, fear moving in his heart. He was disoriented for a moment, not knowing where he was for a moment. On his feet, he searched for his kidnappers. He followed the light from the office to stand and watch his sister. He knew that she was in danger but he didn't know who from or why.

Triese looked around as she heard a sound, frowning. Her frown cleared as she saw Tait there in the doorway. She walked towards him, hugging him and then tugging him into her office. She pushed him down into a chair, seating herself on the floor beside him.

"Tait? What are you thinking?" Triese watched her brother closely, seeing the changes that his captivity had wrought in him and not liking them. She struggled to release those feelings to God, knowing that was what she had to do.

"I don't know, Triese. You're in danger and I don't know why or from whom. That's why I was taken, I think." Tait was distraught at that before his sister began to pray and that prayer relieved some of his fears but not all of them.

Chapter 22

A few days later, Teeg wandered through the wilderness near his home. Andy paced at his side, alert but not reacting to anything. For that, Teeg was grateful. He himself was alert to any wildlife that appeared, stopping as they did with his camera raised to document it. His notebook was in and out of his backpack as he made his notes. He felt something off but was not sure about what it was.

Stopping at a windfall, Teeg waited, knowing that this was usually where a number of critters could be found. He was not disappointed, making his notes and taking his pictures. Reaching for his bottle of water, he drank before he capped it and dropped it back into his pack. Andy had had water as well and Teeg reached for his bowl. His hand stopped as he tucked the folding bowl away, his eyes on the paper that was just visible in the windfall. That had not been there the day before, he knew as he had been that way.

Sighing, Teeg reached for it, finding as he suspected that it was a threat against himself but not Triese. He frowned at that. As far as he knew, he had no enemies. This was puzzling. Teeg tucked away the paper and continued on his way. He had tasks to do and do that day. He would deal with the letter later.

That afternoon, he laid the letter on the table, spread out so that he could read it again. He took a picture of it and sent it on to Toby before he went to change from his work clothes. Returning, he studied the letter again. He was still puzzled at the threat.

Teeg reached for his phone, calling Triese, desperate to hear that she was okay. He could only leave a voice mail, praying that she was fine. He received a quick text message from her, just stating that she was on a conference call and would call him later. A heart symbol accompanied her message. That brought a smile to his face.

Toby stood for a moment and stared at his brother's cabin. He shook his head. How did they place that letter just where Teeg would be working that day? He varied his trails each day. Toby began a systematic search before he found the cameras located near the cabin, one directed at each trail that Teeg walked.

Teeg watched his brother, a frown on his face until he realized what Toby was finding. That disturbed him greatly.

"Toby?" Teeg paced forward to stand beside his brother. Toby was leaning over his car hood, labeling the evidence bags. "There were that many?"

"There were. One pointed to each trail that you would have taken. That's how they knew which trail you would take today. Someone was ahead of you and planted that. Do you have time tomorrow to take me out there? It's too late in the day to do that now." Toby wanted to see the area himself and knew that he would be dragging Roger with him.

"That works. If we leave early, it takes about an hour. That would put us there about the time I reached it today."

"That works. For now, show me the actual letter." Toby stalked towards the cabin to stand in front of the table. He read and reread the letter. "This is brutal, Teeg. What have you gotten mixed up in?"

"I have no idea. It all goes back to Triese. And she doesn't know or remember what would be the case. Tait is at a loss as well. How far have you looked into this Walt?" Teeg eyed his brother.

"We are. We're not getting too far as yet." Toby leaned against the table, holding onto the evidence bag that held the letter.

The next morning, Teeg, Toby, and Roger headed for the windfall. Toby's hand kept Teeg back from it as he and Roger moved in on the windfall. Teeg waited somewhat impatiently as they searched the area and then stood deep in discussion before they walked towards him.

"Teeg? That was all you found? The letter?" Toby was sure of the answer as he knew what his brother had said.

"It is. Was there something more?" Teeg watched as Roger and Toby shared a look before Toby nodded.

"There is. There is some evidence that I can't discuss with you right at the moment. Walk with me while Roger retrieves it." Toby's hand on Teeg's arm drew him away from the windfall.

"I see. Does it affect Triese?" Teeg was worried about her. He had still not had a chance to speak with her even though he had managed to speak with Tait.

"It seems to. We'll get together with both of you and discuss what we can." Toby drew in a deep breath of the fresh air. It was now early September, a favourite time of year. "Teeg, you don't have to answer, but how serious are you about Triese?" Toby didn't look at his brother as he asked the question.

Teeg stopped moving, not sure how to respond. He wasn't sure himself.

"I would like to date her, Toby. You know me. I never date." Teeg looked up at the sky. "I don't know how to answer your question."

"That's okay. I probably shouldn't have asked it and in normal circumstances, I would not have asked. But the circumstances under which you now find yourself? I have to know. That tells me what I need to know. We'll do our best to keep you both safe. But you know that we can't make promises to do that."

"I know that you'll do your best. Unfortunately, your best sometimes isn't enough. God is in control, that I fully believe. He will watch out for us. Whatever happens to us, He already knows about. He walks beside us each step of the way."

"I know that. God is there but I still worry about you and Triese. I wish I could save you from danger, but I can't. I can only do the best that I can to protect you both. At some point, that won't be enough and that scares me, Teeg. I have seen too much."

"I know that you have and you're wearing out under the burden of it all. I wish life was different but it's not." Teeg had watched his brother over the years. "You need a lady, Toby."

“I know. God has one out there for me, if it’s in His will for me.” Toby walked away to where Roger was waiting for him.

Chapter 23

Triese rose from her office chair that afternoon, stretching and then rubbing at the back of her neck. She had been sitting there for hours, not even rising to find something to drink. She headed for the kitchen and reached for a bottle of water. She stared at the food and water bowls, wishing that Andy was there. If Andy was there, then it meant that Teeg was as well. She was missing him greatly.

She headed out into the yard, finding Tait sitting on the back stairs. She sat beside him, not seeing their parents anywhere around.

"Where are Mom and Dad?" Triese kept her voice low. Tait was not comfortable with any loud tones of voice.

"They're out with Teeg's parents, I think. I've been sitting here, trying to figure it all out." Tait tilted his head to study his sister.

"And you're not getting anywhere with that. I'm not either. I told you what happened to me and then to Teeg. It's not making sense. I don't have anything that anyone would want. If there's something in a picture I took, I would have no idea where to start looking. I have too many photos to go over in a quick manner."

"No, you can't do that. I wish that I could figure it out. My life was upended too much." Tait bit at his lip. "What happened to my stuff?"

"Your things? Mom and Dad emptied your apartment and stored your things. Do you want them sent here?" Triese didn't push her brother. He would have to make that decision.

"You're not leaving here, not if Teeg has anything to say about it. I have no desire to go back to our home town. It holds memories of what happened to me, memories that I don't want to relive." Tait sighed, rubbing at his temple with an index finger. "I guess I should have stuff sent here. You're sure you're okay with me living with you?"

"Tait! How can you ask that? You're my brother. Of course, I'm okay with that. You have to live somewhere. Together, we can face what is going on and solve it. God brought you here." She frowned at him. "How did they know?"

"Know what?" Tait was confused.

"How did they know where I was? I had left town before you disappeared and settled here." Triese drew in a deep breath. "Someone was watching me too closely back then. You were brought here because this is where I live. They were going to use you to threaten me. But I don't understand why so long. Did I not do anything that would warrant them threatening me and using you to do that?"

Tait stared at his sister. She had just asked a question that had puzzled him greatly.

"I don't know why they didn't bring me out sooner. I don't know that they had permission to do so. There were times that I heard an older voice outside of my room. I didn't recognize his voice. I wish that I could. That would solve this." Tait rose and paced, his face thoughtful. "How do we prove that, Triese?"

"I don't know how, Tait." She looked around as she heard a voice and then Teeg and Andy appeared. "Teeg? I wasn't expecting you today."

"I had to see you. I had to know that you were okay." Teeg hugged her in almost terrified manner.

Triese stared at Tait as Tait stared back at her.

"Teeg? What is going on?" Triese showed back from him. "What are you talking about?"

"I was out working yesterday and found a threatening letter. Toby, Roger, and I headed back there today. It's brutal, Triese. It threatens me and then you as well. Tait, you were mentioned as well. Someone is watching us too closely for us to take any chances." Teeg refused to let go of his lady.

Tait frowned at him before his head dropped. He was going through his list of friends from years ago to decide who he could reach out to. His head raised once more. He knew who to reach out to.

"Triese? You remember that friend of mine?"

"Which one? You have so many, all of whom were looking for you." She smirked at him as she said that.

"He went to work for the Barnabas Foundation. Brandon. Why don't I reach out to him? You know they went through some pretty rough stuff." He paced away as she thought it through.

"Tait? That would help. They have resources that we don't. Do you still have his number?" Triese reached for her phone, handing it to him. "Here. Use mine. We still need to replace yours."

"I think I do. I can send a message to Barnabas and he'll put me in touch with Brandon." Tait walked away to make his call. He prayed that Barnabas would be able to help them. He was disappointed to only be able to leave a voice mail but he knew that either Barnabas or Brandon would reach out to him.

"You know the people from the Barnabas Foundation?" Teeg had not been aware of that.

"We do. Brandon was a friend of Tait's until he moved near here to take work with the Barnabas Foundation. We've kept in touch over the years. I know that the men and ladies from that group have been helping us look for him." Triese leaned against Teeg, revelling in how safe she felt with him. "Teeg? What is Andy doing?" She pointed towards the dog.

"Andy? He's doing what he was trained to do. He's checking out your property for anything that might harm you. And if he finds anything that he doesn't like, he will sit." Teeg watched Andy closely. "So far, he's not alerting to anything."

"He does that? You've trained him well." Triese turned to face him. "It's suppertime. I need to find something for us to eat."

Teeg grinned at her.

“You have a grill. Do you have anything that we can grill?” He refused to let her go, dropping a kiss on her forehead instead.

Triese stared up at him. Had he really just done that?

“I do. I took hamburger patties out this morning, thinking that Tait might like that. He had a very bland diet, he tells me, for two years. I am trying to give him a variety of meals.” She freed herself to walk into the house.

Teeg turned his head as he heard Tait’s voice beside him.

“What was that you said to Triese?”

“About the letter? I found it yesterday on a windfall when I was out on one of my trails. It threatened all of us.”

“That’s what I am afraid of. I don’t want to see Triese hurt and I know that I can’t stop whatever I’m going through. I wish that I could.” Tait was sober as he stated that, Teeg knowing how he felt to some degree.

Chapter 24

Tait ran for the house the next morning, looking for Triese. She had called for him and then was silent. He slid to a halt in her office, watching as Triese stared back at him before she was handing him her phone.

"It's Brandon. He's glad to hear you're safe but he does have some questions for you." Triese walked away, knowing that Tait needed that privacy. She squinted at the clock, sighing to herself. It was only mid-morning but felt so much later. Reaching for the coffee pot, Triese stared at the remains of the pot that had been brewed earlier before she dumped it out and made fresh. She then paced to the outside as she waited for the coffee to finish brewing.

Tait found her at last, handing her back her phone. He needed to get his own and was planning on asking Triese to help him get one that day.

"Tait? What did Brandon have to say?" Triese was not prying but she did need to know if it affected her.

"Not a lot. He took what information that I could give him. He's going to reach out to you as well, to see what you can tell him about what you're going through. I don't have enough information to tell him that." Tait was frustrated by that.

"I'll call him then, Tait. For now, we need to find you that phone. Come on. I'm done with what I need to do today." Triese locked her home and headed for her car. She paused. "Tait, you need to renew your license, don't you?"

"I need to get one for here. I'm not moving from Ontario. You're staying here and I don't want to move away from you." He was sober as he said that.

"Thank you, Tait. I don't want you to move away either. But you do need to learn to live your life again. You've found someone to speak with?" At Tait's nod, she relaxed.

An hour later, they were seated in a diner, waiting for their meal. Tait looked around. He felt out of place being out there, but Triese had insisted. He noted that she seemed to be well known as different people waved or spoke to her. She was quick to introduce him as her brother and he was welcomed as well. He had to get used to this once more.

Teeg stopped as he entered the diner. He had been out in the wilderness that morning and had decided that he didn't want to cook. He had headed to his favourite diner, stopping just inside the door as he looked for a seat. Teeg was surprised to see Tait, who was watching him and then looking across the table at someone. He headed that way, not surprised to see Triese. He sat beside her, causing her to jump and stare at him with eyes that were huge with fear. He simply grinned at her.

Triese stared at Teeg before her eyes narrowed. She could hear Tait trying to stifle his laughter. She shifted over on her seat to give Teeg more room. She didn't want to be there all of a sudden but she had no way to escape.

Conversation was varied and yet sprinkled with laughter. Tait was beginning to relax some, knowing that God was working in his life and bringing that about. He watched the couple across from him, seeing what Toby had said. They were a couple, he decided. Tait was happy for his sister. He just wished that it had been under different circumstances.

Teeg reached for Triese's hand as they walked from the diner. Tait reached for Triese's keys and with a wave, he headed for her car. Triese stared after him, frowning at how he had just left her there.

Teeg began to laugh, causing Triese to frown at him in turn.

"He left you, darling. I guess that means I drive you home." He walked her over to his truck and tucked her inside before jumping behind the wheel.

"I guess. I wish that he had not done that. I feel very vulnerable right now, and things like what Tait did? That makes it worse." She buried her face in her hands. "I'm sorry. I know that he meant well but I can't handle this right now."

Teeg reached to wrap an arm around her. He could see how affected that she was.

"He did mean well. We are a couple, Triese, whether we want to be or not at the present time. We've been pushed into something that we don't want. I would not want to not have you in my life. I don't know where we're heading, Triese, but I do know that my life would be bereft without you." Teeg watched her closely.

Triese had turned to watch him before she nodded. She felt the same way.

"Where do we go with the investigation, Teeg? Tait has reached out to a friend and I know that all of that group will work on it." She hesitated. "Are you familiar with the Barnabas Foundation?"

"I am." He studied her for a moment before his face cleared. "You're friends with them?"

"One of them. Brandon was a friend with Tait when they were younger. They have kept in touch over the years. Brandon was really worried when Tait was missing. They have all tried to find him."

"I see. And he's going to help with this?"

"He is. Tait spoke with him this morning. Only, I don't know what they'll find, if anything." Triese stared out of the window as Teeg drove towards her home. "How do we find the ones responsible?"

"Toby is working on that. He'll want to talk with the three of us soon." Teeg pulled into her driveway and turned off his truck. "In the meantime, we need to take all the precautions that we can."

"I get that, Teeg. I just don't have to like it." Triese was sober as she spoke but also disgruntled. She didn't like that she was under attack from someone unknown.

"No, we don't have to like it. And God understands how we feel." Teeg walked around the truck to help her out of it. "How's Tait?"

Triese shrugged. She was unable to read how her brother was really doing. That was a change for her, and she blamed his captivity.

Chapter 25

Toby walked towards his brother's cabin the next afternoon. A hand went out to greet Andy who had run towards him, his tail wagging his body. Toby bent over, rubbing the dog who was loving every moment of it. Straightening back up, he stared around him. He didn't feel any danger that evening which was a relief.

Teeg stood near his cabin, watching his brother. He didn't know why Toby was here but he prayed that it wasn't about the investigation. He was at a loss regarding that.

"Toby? You're here? Not with bad news, I pray."

"No, not this time. I just wanted to spend some time with you. There have been some promising leads but I don't have enough information to go over anything with you." Toby rested a hand on his brother's shoulder. "What are you planning for a meal?"

"A meal? I hadn't thought that far ahead. I just got back home." Teeg turned in a circle. "I don't feel anyone watching me tonight, and I have been every night."

"That's good." Teeg pushed his brother towards the cabin. "Let's eat and then spend some time in prayer. Are you meeting with Triese tonight?"

Teeg shook his head. He had wanted to but Triese and Tait had plans with their parents. He was worried about her and then there was Tait. He didn't seem to be doing as well as he had been.

"Not tonight. She's with her parents. It's Tait that is concerning. He's regressing, I think."

"He will." Toby paused as he set the coffee to drip. "Has he found someone to speak with?"

"He has. A friend from the Barnabas Foundation. Buckley used to be their pastor but now works with victims of crime. He and Locklin went through an adventure as they said. She almost died from a deliberate drug overdose that was administered to her. Triese says he's depressed and worried. She's worried in turn about him." Teeg sighed. "This isn't working out so well."

"No, it's not. You want to protect her but you can't in the way that you want to." Toby turned to his brother. "There are just so many unknowns right now. And neither of us can understand who or why. Do you have any ideas?"

Teeg shrugged. He had so many ideas that he had covered many pages with them. He reached for the copy that he had for his brother.

"Here. This is a copy for you. I don't know that I've got it down in any sort of order. More or less, it's just ramblings. And that's not me." Teeg was very organized in his thoughts and writings. For him to admit this? Toby knew then how upset and worried his brother was.

“I’ll look through it.” Toby stared down at his sandwich, setting it back on the plate. “You mentioned the Barnabas Foundation?”

Teeg nodded, with a slight grin on his face. He had been waiting for Toby to ask.

“Brandon who works with them is a friend of Tait’s. Tait has reached out to him to ask for help. They have resources that no one really knows about, from what Triese says. And I can see that.” Teeg bit into his sandwich and chewed before he swallowed. He reached for his coffee mug and swallowed a mouthful. “I pray that they find something that will help.”

“I am sure that they will. Anyone who can help is welcome. Did you hear from Richard or his security team?”

“I heard from Stephen. He’s planning on coming around in the next few days and bringing his wife with him. That will help Triese, I think. She feels isolated by this and that can’t continue. She needs to understand that others have had these types of events.” Teeg dropped his sandwich on his plate, his appetite gone.

Toby watched his brother, frowning at him. He had not expected Teeg to react this way.

"How do I help her, Toby? What can I do for her? I want to find these men and bring them to justice. I know that God is our Shield but they seem to be able to get around that."

"And they are doing that because God has allowed it. Now, I need to ask you something personal, Teeg. You don't need to answer if you don't want to." Toby eyed his brother, seeing the stress and strain and worry that was uppermost in his brother's mind and heart at the moment. "How close are you to Triese?"

"How close am I?" Teeg waited for a moment, praying through his answer. He knew what he wanted to say but that declaration had to go to Triese first. He did not want to lose the lady who had become so important to him. He was just afraid that circumstances would drive her away. "I love her, Toby, and yes, I have told her that. She has not responded, not that I expected her to. She's got a lot going on right now, with what we're involved in and then with Tait reappearing. It's strange, you know. Just how did he get away and why now?" Teeg was genuinely puzzled by that.

"I know, Teeg. Those are questions that we don't have any answers for. Not yet at any rate. Tait can't say. He didn't see anyone who had released him but he did say a man helped him once he was out of the house. And he can't even tell me where the house was. He's not familiar with that area but it was near here, we suspect." Toby rose to clear the table and then bring out the apple pie that his mother had given Teeg. A hand reached to rub at Andy's ears as he passed the dog.

"It is bizarre, Toby. We can't trace his steps. He can't tell us how to do that. And this man? What do we know about him?" Teeg looked hopeful at that.

"Nothing. Tait can't remember much about him." Toby grinned suddenly. "Your lady is convinced that the man was an angel."

Teeg looked thoughtful at that. Somehow, he suspected that Triese was correct.

"It could well be, you know. God does that. I've heard of it happening before. In fact, Tait mentioned one of the men from the Barnabas Foundation. The man's wife, Muir, had someone involved in her life and her granny's life that they both swear was an angel. He was there and then would disappear."

Toby was nodding. He had heard the same over the years from other victims of crime.

"It would not surprise me. God has promised to protect us, and I firmly believe that sometimes He does just that. Send an angel to protect us and help us."

Chapter 26

Triese walked through her home, not sure why she was so distressed that morning. Tait was out with their parents and she was glad for that. He had changed over the past two years. She didn't think that she knew him any more. That was not what she had prayed for over the years that she had been apart from her brother. But it was expected, she knew. It had to be. Tait could not remain the same as he had been.

Turning as she heard the doorbell, she crept that way, standing back so that she could see out of the door window without being seen. Triese frowned. Brit was there but she didn't know the lady with her.

Opening the door, Triese was not surprised to have Brit hug her and then hold on for a bit before she stepped back.

"Triese? Are we interrupting your work?" Brit had been worried about that.

"No, you're not. I have some photos to work on but nothing urgent. You're here, though?" Triese headed for the kitchen, an eye on the clock. "It's lunchtime, you know."

"I know. We brought food." Brit bit at her lip. "Triese, let me introduce you to this lady. This is Muir, Burnie's wife. He works for the Barnabas Foundation with victims of crime. You need to hear their story. I know that Tait is friends with Brandon and the others."

"He is. I have heard him mention your name in the past few days. Mutter it would be more like it." Triese grinned at Muir. "Welcome to my home." Her hands reached to help put out their meal.

"It is nice to meet you, Triese. Brandon has mentioned you and did ask if either I or one of the other ladies would be willing to come and speak with you. I know that he and Hagen are heading this way."

"With the twins? I am so eager to meet them. Tait mentioned them the other day." Triese sighed as she found her seat. "Can we pray first, ladies? I know that we're doing that but I just know that things are heating up as they say. God is the only one who can protect us."

"We can do that, Triese. Buckley was the pastor for our church until he took on a new duty with the Foundation. He misses that contact with his people, as he calls them, but God had this plan for him and Locklin all along. What Burnie and I went through did help us in understanding to some extent what other victims are going through. And you are a victim, Triese, whether you are willing to acknowledge that or not So is Teeg and your brother. You are not alone in this, We have covered you all in prayer. Now, let's pray and eat. Then you can ask anything that you need to know the answer for."

Triese nodded, knowing that she had many questions. It was just whether she could or would ask them.

Late that afternoon, Tait approached his sister, his head tilting to study her. Something had happened that day, he could tell. He wanted to talk with her but given the gap in their history, he was unsure how to proceed.

"Triese? Are you okay?" Tait reached to hug his sister, feeling that both of them needed that contact.

"I am, I think. Brit was here today. She had Burnie's Muir with her." Triese studied her brother, seeing understanding in his eyes. "I didn't know that they had all gone through danger like that. Muir had an interesting comment."

"And that would be?" Tait was puzzled at his sister's words.

"She is adamant that she had an angel watching out for herself and her granny." Triese knew that was possible. She just had not run into anyone who had had that happen to them.

"She did, Triese. I firmly believe it. And I think the man who rescued me was an angel as well." Tait paced, not able to seat himself and stay still. "I hate this, Triese. You're in danger as is Teeg. That's because of you. I disappeared for two years and lost that time with my family that we'll never get back. And there was no reason given for that. I went those two years not talking to a human being at all. Even when I tried to escape, they were silent."

"It was part of how they tried to beat you down and destroy you. It didn't work. You talked with God instead." Triese watched her brother closely, seeing the changes that she hated to see but also seeing how strong his faith had become over the years. "Sometimes, He does that, draws us aside. I hate that it had to be that way for you." She looked around. "And just where are our parents?"

"They're off with Teeg's parents. Something about a dinner meeting at the church. I'm glad that they have that support here." Tait walked away to find his bed. Even though it was still early afternoon, he was exhausted. The physician who had examined him told him to expect that. He had to learn how to live as a free man once more. And that would be exhausting.

Teeg turned from staring at the street as the door behind him opened. He simply swept Triese into a hug, feeling the sobs that she was suppressing shaking her body. Seeing her keys on the table in the entryway, he reached for them, locked the door, and then with her hand tight in his, led her away from the house and towards a nearby park. He found a bench not quite in the open and seated them both. His arm wrapped around her and kept her tight to him.

"Talk to me, darling. What's going on? Did something else happen today?" Teeg was very worried about his lady.

"No, not really. Your sister stopped in for lunch and had Muir from the Barnabas Foundation with her." Triese leaned into Teeg, not wanting to move from where she felt safe and secure. "How was your day?"

Teeg shrugged. His day had been as usual, he informed her. He had missed her all day. His gaze was directed toward the other side of the park and he frowned. He blinked and the man that he was sure had been watching them had disappeared. He shrugged, not thinking anything about it.

"Teeg? What are your thoughts today about all this? I don't understand it at all." Triese was grasping at straws, hoping that Triese might have an answer for her.

"I really don't know what to think. I've gone over all the tasks and work that I have done over the past few years. Nothing stands out to me that would cause this. And have you been able to go over any of your photos?"

"Not yet, but I do need to. There are just too many." Triese was sober as she spoke.

"How be we meet this Saturday and start going over the ones for about a year before Tait disappeared. Brit and Toby will help and I have other friends who I can call in to help."

"That works Tait is away with Dad that day but Mom will help. She has an eye for catching things that I miss."

"That happens. It's hard going back over your own work. We'll plan on that." Teeg reluctantly rose and reached for her hand. "Let's get you home, darling. And I do love you."

Chapter 27

Early Saturday morning, Triese was on her feet. She had baked the day before and brought in food. Tait had grinned at her and then simply helped. They worked together as they had when they were younger. Tait was sorry not to be there but he needed the time alone with his father. He had missed his words, prayers, and counsel for too long, he had decided.

Abygayle approached Triese as she arrived, coming in the early morning as well. She had hugged her daughter, feeling the tension in her.

"Triese? What can I do for you?" Abygayle looked around, seeing the organization that Triese was noted for.

"I don't know, Mom. I'm not sure that this will solve anything today. I have borrowed a couple of laptops and I know that more are on their way. How do I let go of my work and let someone else search it?" Triese had been deeply troubled at the thought.

"You do it with God's help, love. He is the One who will use your friends and family to look through the photos. I spoke with Teeg last night. He called me, just to ask how we were. Hold on to that man, Triese." She grinned at her daughter, seeing her daughter's mouth open and close in surprise. "I mean that. He is a wonderful and thoughtful man. Now, we have been praying over this for days now. God will lead us in the search, I have no doubt about that. And before you say anything, everyone is aware of how many photos you have. Teeg has suggested that we break them into months, with a group taking a month. And yes, there will be enough to do that. That way, we're not overwhelmed trying to do a full year. He also suggested that once we have gone through a year, that you tell us which year to do next. We can either move to an earlier year or come to a later year. It will be your decision where we search and yours alone. I know how much you dislike this but you are going out of your comfort zone to try and solve it."

That afternoon, Triese rose and walked away from her desk. She needed a break. She felt that they had accomplished a lot. She was just not used to the crowd of people in her home. Triese turned as she stepped outside, finding Andy beside her. The dog stood up to kiss her face, accepting the hug that the lady gave him.

Triese was thoughtful as she studied her home. Teeg's parents, his brother, sister, and uncle had shown up. Her mother had been there of course. And also a security team run by someone named Richard had turned up with the four men and women on his team and their spouses. Muir and her husband Burnie, an author, had also shown up. She had studied Burnie, finding it interesting how he worked. Muir had grinned at her, simply stating that Burnie would work it as a plot line in one of his mystery stories. Triese had returned her grin, knowing that it would be interesting what he found.

Tyler had watched Truese walk away before he was on his feet to follow her. He closed the door quietly, a hand out for Andy to lick at.

"Triese? How are you doing?" Tyler's voice held concern for her.

Tries shrugged. She had no idea how she was to feel. Not any more. At one time, she would have been quick to respond. She looked up at the uncle of the man who she now acknowledged that she loved.

"I really don't know any more, Tyler. Does that make sense?" She watched as he sat near her.

"It does and it is normal. It's what all victims say." Tyler bit at his lip for a moment. "Triese, have you ever been threatened at all over your work? Has anyone ever been hostile towards you?"

Triese thought through that. She shook her head and then paused, a frown on her face.

"There was one person, about three years ago, who was hostile. I never did do any photos for him. It would have meant travelling to Europe and I wasn't prepared to do that. I have enough here in Canada and the United States to keep me busy. I don't even remember his name. I didn't keep any contact information on him. At least, I don't think that I did." She was on her feet, almost running for her office. Tyler followed her, watching as Andy ran beside her.

Triese startled the ones at work in her office, causing heads to raise. Teeg dropped what he was doing and was on his feet, a hand on her arm.

"What happened, darling?"

"I need to check to see if I have contact information on someone who I refused to do any work for. Tyler asked me that question. Who had threatened or been hostile towards me. There was someone about three or four years ago." Triese was frantically searching her filing cabinet before her hand froze. Her eyes closed as she thanked God that she still had that information. She shouldn't have kept it but she had. And she had no idea why.

Tyler reached for the folder and opened it to read the name and contact information and what the man had wanted from Triese. He silently passed it over to Toby who read it as well. The two officers shared a look. This might just be the lead that they wanted.

Triese turned to face the room, finding all of the people present there looking at her with concern on each face. She sighed. This is not what she wanted, but she had not given it a thought when she ran into the room. She felt Teeg's arms around her and leaned back against him.

"It's okay. I found a name to give Tyler. If anyone recognizes, let me know." She said the name, her eyes on Richard as she did so. She caught the faint nod that he gave and was determined that she would speak with him at some point, either that day or another day. He had information that she needed.

"How be we take a break, people?" Stephen was on his feet, a question on his face. It was near to suppertime and he had no idea what was planned.

"I have meat that can be grilled, Stephen. And with what you all brought, we have salads and sides enough for a meal. I can't thank you enough." Tears sparkled briefly in her eyes. "You all have been the hands and feet of God today."

"That's what we do, Triese." Naomi, one of Richard's team members, spoke up. "We can understand to a certain extent how you feel. But don't let anyone ever tell you that they know exactly how you feel. It is just not possible. God leads us each on our own unique paths."

"That He does. He knows just how much we can handle with His care." Burnie leaned forward, elbows planted on his knees. "I have come up with some wild plot lines but none of them have ever come close to what we all faced."

"I gather that, Burnie. Thank you for your words." Triese was suddenly exhausted. Her body sagged back against Teeg before she straightened up. "Let's eat and then see if we need to come back to this. I know that you have all been making notes over the day. I can't thank you enough for what you have done. If someone would make copies for each of us, that would help." Triese walked away at that, Stephen beside her and Toby on her other side.

The men joked around with her, causing her to set aside her worries and smile. She knew what they were up to and appreciated it. She looked up once as she was setting out the salads and found Teeg watching her, a thoughtful look on his face which turned into a smile just for her.

Chapter 28

Walking towards the church the next morning, Teeg hit the key fob to lock his truck doors. He could see Triese waiting for him, and his face softened. They had parted mid-evening the night before, with him being the last to leave her. He had sensed that something had changed in their relationship, something for the better, but Teeg would not question her. Not yet, any way.

"All set, darling?" Teeg reached for her hand.

"I am. Thank you for being who you are, Teeg. Your support and prayers have meant a lot." Triese was not looking at him as she spoke. Instead, her attention was on a vehicle that was driving slowly through the parking lot. Sudden fear had her tugging Teeg into the church to where she could watch out of a window.

"Triese? What just happened?" Teeg was puzzled as he watched Toby approaching them.

Toby took one look at Triese and then was out of the door, his uncle on his heels. They scoured the parking lot before Toby pointed toward the car that had caught Triese's attention.

"That car, Uncle Ty. There's something off about it."

"And it's parked right beside Teeg's truck."

The two men walked towards it, careful not to startle anyone or touch the vehicle. Toby leaned forward to study the interior as much as he could. He could hear his uncle muttering to himself that he was too old for this. The "this" had to be getting down on his knees and searching under the car. Tyler was on his feet, pulling Toby away from the car and then pulling out his phone. He sighed. He really wanted to be in church that morning and needed the message and the contact with his fellow church members. That was apparently not going to happen.

Ed walked towards Tyler from the church. He had stopped beside Teeg who had shrugged. Teeg had been unable to convince Triese to enter the sanctuary. Instead, her attention was on the activity in the parking lot.

Teeg stepped outside, a finger pointed at Triese to stay put. He knew that she wouldn't. Instead, she stepped outside beside him, his arm wrapped around her.

"Teeg? What is going on?" Triese kept her voice very low. She didn't know why she did that. It just seemed the right thing to do.

"I would suspect that something is off with the car. They didn't ask Ed to step in for nothing." Teeg turned as he heard the door open and close behind him. He was somewhat surprised to see Richard standing nearby. "Richard?"

"It's okay, Teeg. We're all here today again. The team wanted to. They're worried about you two for some reason." Richard grinned at them for a moment before he sobered. "And from what is happening over there, I would suspect that their concerns are correct."

"More than likely." Teeg had no idea what was happening. All he knew was that his lady was disturbed and that disturbed him. He was finding it hard to trust God in all this. The blackness and darkness seemed to be closing in on him.

"It is hard to trust, Teeg. I've been there. Just because I run a security team doesn't mean I have all the answers. I don't. Now, how be we get you two back inside? You're vulnerable out here. And you do need to hear at least part of the message." Richard shoved them back inside and then into a seat near the back of the church. He then stood behind them, his back against the wall.

Toby approached the church, his mind not on his brother for the moment but on what they had discovered. Ed and his team had removed the bomb from the vehicle and disarmed it. That took that particular worry away. But they had no idea who the car belonged to. The plates had been removed and the vehicle identification number had been destroyed. They were at a loss, he knew, unless someone recognized it. And he wasn't putting any of his hopes on that.

Timothy and Silver, two more of Richard's team, approached him.

"Toby? What can you tell us? We want to make sure that those two get away from her safely." Silver's voice was quiet so as not to worry anyone around her.

"There was a bomb which has been removed. The car has been towed. I just don't know what to think. There are these threats but we can't find anyone behind them. Both Teeg and Triese can't come up with any other names."

"And you need that or at least to find someone who will talk. This person is staying very well hidden. He seems to know what you are doing." Timothy had seen this before.

"We've both seen this too many times. I want whoever it is. Teeg and Triese can't go on with their lives until we do. Tait needs to heal and can't fully without knowing why. Their parents are hurting as well." Silver spoke the truth.

"We all do. And I just don't see where to turn next." Toby walked away, leaving the other two lost in thought.

"Silver? What are your thoughts?"

"I don't know, Timothy. I really don't know. I want this over for Teeg and Triese. I just don't see it happening." Silver snapped her fingers. "Emma!"

"Emma? Of course. I wonder if anyone has reached out to her." Timothy turned slightly as he heard a throat clear. "Titus?"

"This Emma? She's that friend of yours who finds people and things?" Titus grinned at them as they both nodded. "Someone gave her my number. She called me this morning. I gave her what I could and she's working on it. I pray that she does find something and soon." Titus walked away to find his sons. He needed to do that. Both of his sons were hurting and not living the joy-filled life that they had been. He wanted that to change and change quickly.

Triese was on edge all the rest of the day. Even when she crawled into her bed and pulled the covers over her, she was shaking. To hear that a bomb had been placed in such a manner had disturbed her greatly. She was not prepared for that. Teeg had held her as she had tried to comprehend what danger that had meant. She didn't like it and knew that he didn't either. This adventure that they seemed to be sharing was testing them and not just in their faith. It was testing their fortitude and strength of character. It was also playing havoc with how they viewed people around them and their motives. Triese was not sure that she would ever trust anyone completely again. That trust in humanity had been destroyed over the past few weeks and she had to admit it was destroyed over the past few years.

Teeg drew a blanket around him as he found a spot on the couch. He was not ready to sleep and didn't know when he would be. Andy had jumped up beside him, trying to bring comfort as only he could. Tonight, that comfort was not there and Teeg was dismayed at that. He prayed for a resolution of their adventure, not sure when or if it would ever be over.

Chapter 29

Toby paced towards where he could see Triese standing outside of a store. She was in danger and yet was out and about. He could not fault her for that. Triese had turned as she heard the footsteps thudding towards her, her face paling as she saw the grim look on Toby's face.

"Toby? What happened? Is it Teeg? Is he okay? No, not Tait! Not again!" Triese was almost incoherent with her words, her worry for both men uppermost in her thoughts.

Toby slowed his footsteps, mentally berating himself. He shouldn't have approached her so quickly but he had been worried. He had been by her house and not found her. He had been driving through the downtown area when he spied her.

"They're fine, Triese. I'm sorry. I didn't mean to frighten you." With his hand on her arm, Toby looked around, pointing towards a small cafe nearby. "Here. In there. I do need to speak with you but first I would like to share a coffee with a lady who is very special to my brother." He grinned at her frown.

"Is that so? Well, then, I guess you must." She smirked at him, causing him to laugh. She had accomplished what she wanted.

Their coffee was low in their mugs when Triese raised her head. Her eyes were thoughtful as she watched Toby. That he was uncomfortable was obvious.

"Toby? What did you need to tell me?" Triese went right to the point.

"Direct and to the point. I like that. Does Teeg know that you do that?" Toby grinned at her again before he sobered. "We do need to talk, Triese. This is an okay place, I guess. Just how are you doing right now? And don't tell me that you're fine. You're not."

"No, I'm not." Triese was willing to admit that. "But that's not what you want to say or ask."

"No, it's not. That name that you gave us? We've tracked him down." Toby was hesitant to continue but he knew that he had to.

At his hesitation, Triese stared at him before she stared down at the hand with which she was rubbing the tablecloth.

"He's dead, isn't he?" Her voice was barely above a whisper. She didn't look up at Toby. She was afraid to see what would be on his face.

"He is, Triese. I'm sorry. I was praying that he would have some answers for you. And his death is suspicious. They have never been able to solve how he died." Toby waited for the questions to come, but Triese didn't ask any. "Triese?"

"It's okay, Toby. It was too much to hope that he would have answers for us. That's a dead end now." Triese was on her feet, money dropped on the table for her meal, brushing by Toby who had also risen to his feet.

Toby dropped money on the table as well and then followed Triese. By the time he reached the sidewalk, Triese had disappeared. He searched for her before he headed for his car. He had another crime scene to get to, according to the text message that he had just received. Reaching the scene, he was shocked to see one of the suspects from Triese's kidnapping, the one that set everything in the beginning of her adventure. Toby took the note that was encased in the evidence bag. He was shocked to see that it was addressed to Tait.

"This was found here?"

"It was." Roger shook his head. "What next with those two? Can't they just have a normal life like everyone else?"

Toby gave a grim smile. He shared those sentiments. He had no idea what all they were involved with. He wanted this over for his brother and his lady and the lady's brother. It just didn't seem to be happening.

Teeg paced the clearing that he had stopped in He was puzzled by what he had found. There should have been no signs of any people but he could tell that someone had been there. Andy was on edge and searching. Teeg watched as Andy continued to search the area. He turned and walked back to the trees, his backpack dropped there for a moment. Hearing a yelp from Andy, Teeg spun, ready to run towards him. He stopped, his hands rising in the air. He looked around the two men facing him to see that Andy had been restrained with a tool used by animal control to contain dogs. Andy was fighting the man until Teeg's yell had him sitting. Andy kept his eyes on the man, ready to attack if he found an opportunity to do so.

Teeg's attention went back to the two men. He heard a soft sound behind him before he was forcibly shoved onto the stump of a tree. He landed heavily, a groan coming from him. His attention did not leave the men in front of him. He couldn't look away. Teeg could hear the soft whines coming from Andy but there was nothing that he could do for his beloved dog except wait.

Hours seemed to pass as Teeg waited. He shifted uncomfortably and somewhat impatiently on the stump. He had been allowed to take water to Andy and then for himself before he was forced back to his seat. The men had not left the clearing. Teeg frowned at that. It seemed as if they were waiting for something and he had no idea what that something was.

One of the men paced away from the others, his phone out. The call that they had been expecting had come through. He turned to keep an eye on Teeg, puzzled that the man was just sitting there, not making an effort to escape. They had allowed Andy to be free at last, realizing that the dog would not attack them. Andy had settled at Teeg's feet, his eyes watchful. He was ready to attack if Teeg gave the word or if Teeg himself was attacked.

Teeg was uneasy. He looked down at Andy for a moment before he searched the sky. The clouds were moving in and night was coming down as well. He realized that he would not be attending the promised meal with his family and Triese and her family. That saddened him. He didn't want to worry her but he had no choice at this time. It didn't seem as if that would be happening, not that night.

Teeg looked up again, his heart opening to his Heavenly Father. He was the only One who could work this through and let him obtain his freedom.

Chapter 30

Teeg was hauled to his feet an hour later. His hand rested on Andy's head as the dog growled at the men. He didn't like that they were not heading back towards his cabin. Forced to walk towards the other side of the clearing, Teeg frowned. He had an idea where they were heading and he didn't like it one bit. He turned his head, hoping that he and Andy could make a break for it but that wasn't possible. The two men behind him were too close and too much on guard. Teeg sighed to himself as he followed the man leading the group.

Andy paced at Teeg's side, his eyes watchful as well. Every so often, a growl would come from him. He looked up at Teeg, not seeing the command to attack that he was expecting to receive.

Teeg stopped as the man in front of him did so. It was dusk and hard to see in the forest. The men pulled out their flashlights but before they could turn them off, Teeg bent over Andy and sent him away. He had told him to go home. Andy stared at his master but with the command to go home quietly repeated, the dog slunk away, keeping to cover as much as he could. The men didn't notice that the dog had disappeared. They were too concerned with being in the dark in the forest. They were city dwellers who hated the forest.

Forced to walk forward once more, Teeg stumbled for a moment. The debris on the trail that the men had chosen to walk on was deep. He carefully placed one foot down and then the other. His eyes watched as the men struggled as well to move forward. This was not what he had expected today. Not at all. His backpack shifted slightly and Teeg looked around. He was sure that he had felt a hand on his back but the men were too far away. Besides, they would not be helping him. That much he knew. He shrugged and continued to walk forward until he was once more forced to a halt. Teeg stared around, knowing where he was and just how far that they had walked. He shivered slightly in the cool night air and then looked around once more. He didn't feel safe, not one bit.

The three men huddled together, their voices low but angry. They had not expected to be kept out here overnight and were ill prepared for it. The oldest of the men searched and then pointed towards a cabin that was barely visible. He stalked off that way, returning in a short while and directly heading for the men.

Teeg watched their animated and angry conversation before he looked around. Their attention was not on him. He stood and stretched, giving the impression that he needed to do that to relieve his stiffness. He kept an eye on the men and gradually stepped sideways towards shelter. He knew the area, knew the cabin the man had investigated, and knew just how to escape. Teeg didn't think that these men were too wilderness savvy or have enough brain cells as he termed it to figure out how to get out of the area in the dark. It was no problem for him. He had often walked these paths at night with only the stars and moon for light. At times, he didn't even have that.

Moving cautiously through the brush, Teeg set each foot down carefully to avoid any noise or as much as he could. His hands moved aside the branches as he headed directly away from the clearing and then turned towards his home. He paused a few times to swig at the water form his bottle, frowning that it was growing short. He sighed. He had at least a three-hour walk ahead of him, in the dark, with danger around him. Teeg listened carefully but could not hear the men. That surprised him. He was still close enough that he should be able to hear their angry voices. He was not aware that officers had moved in on them and surrounded them. The men had been forced to surrender.

Toby looked around, searching for his brother and not seeing him. They had received word of the abduction from someone on the street and a team had headed for the cabin. Another team had headed for Teeg's cabin, not finding him but finding Andy. Andy was agitated and kept running towards the trees and back. The officers shared a look, all shrugged, and then they followed Andy, knowing that the dog would lead them to Teeg if possible.

Drawing near to his cabin a few hours later, Teeg paused and leaned against a tree. He was exhausted. He had no idea where those men were. And he was worried about Andy. He knew that Andy would have headed home. He just wasn't sure that Andy would have stayed here.

Hearing a soft nod, Teeg crouched down as low as he could get, his hand resting against the rough bark of an oak tree. He listened carefully, a frown on his face before he heard the soft nose getting louder. A whine caught at his hearing and he sank to the ground in relief. He didn't care that the dew was heavy and he would end up with wet clothing. His arms reached to hug Andy as the dog quietly whined and then wriggled around Teeg to lick at any spot of bare flesh that he could find. Teeg looked up to see Toby staring down at him before Toby was hauling him to his feet.

Toby waited patiently as Teeg tended to his dog and then took a shower and found clean and dry clothes. He worked on a quick meal for them of bacon, eggs, and toast. The meal and the fresh coffee were ready by the time Teeg padded into the kitchen in bare feet. He nodded at his brother as he sat, exhaustion uppermost.

Toby waited for Teeg to eat and then rose to clear the table. He refreshed their mugs of coffee before pointing towards the living room area. Teeg staggered for a moment as he stood and Toby's hand came out to steady him. Dropping to the couch, Teeg wrapped an arm around Andy who had jumped up tight to him. His eyes were on Toby. They had not spoken over their meal other than for the blessing. Teeg was having difficulty keeping his eyes open but he needed to talk.

"Teeg? What happened? I got here and found Andy but not you. He kept wanting to head into the forest." Toby waited patiently for his brother to speak.

"I know. I sent him home. This is what happened." Teeg spoke at length, giving his brother every detail that he could remember. He described the men and said where he ended up.

"The Miller cabin? We were warned that someone had planned to take you there. I headed here, hoping to find you but found Andy instead. Other officers were heading for the cabin. I understand that they have arrested the three men."

"They have? That's good news. I hope that they talk and spill the beans on whoever it is that is after either myself, Triese, or Tait." Teeg frowned at Toby. "Toby? Can I ask you something?"

"Sure. What is it?" Toby watched his brother closely. He was very worried about him but could not smother him. They had never been able to do that. Teeg had always demanded that he be allowed to stand on his own two feet, even as a toddler. His family had learned quickly to let him. That independence was still strong even in the face of the danger that he was in.

"What if it wasn't Tait? Or Triese? What if it was someone outside of their family? Someone that they were close to and by going after Tait or Triese, whoever it is thinks that they can get to this person?" Teeg was grasping at the proverbial straw.

"I hear you, Teeg. We are expanding our investigation to those around them. We have a few interesting possibilities that I can't discuss. Tait, Triese, and their parents will be interviewed. Uncle Tyler is arranging for someone other than me to do that, just so I don't taint the case." Toby drew in a deep breath, his eyes closing for a moment. He was exhausted as well, not knowing where or when this would end. Today had been one of those days for him before word came about Teeg's danger. He had been sent to find his brother and he had done that. He just needed to figure out who and why and keep Teeg and Triese safe at the same time. Right now, that seemed to be an insurmountable task.

Chapter 31

The next morning, Teeg was on his feet. He still felt stiff and sore and somewhat disoriented. He had spent a long time in prayer the night before, most of it in just waiting. He was still puzzled by the hand that he had felt on his back. There had been no one there but someone had touched him. Was it the angel that Triese was sure God had provided for her?

Andy paced around Teeg, almost tripping him at times. The dog had not been pleased at all when Teeg had sent him away the day before but he had been trained to follow his master's orders. That man stared at Andy before he smiled. He needed to find his lady and being that it was Saturday, he would do just that. He just didn't know where he would find them.

Triese was restless. She had been burdened for Teeg the afternoon before and that had carried well into the night before she slept, her prayers rising for her knight. She had no idea why she felt the burden but God had impressed on her that she needed to pray for him. Hearing her doorbell ring, Triese hesitated, fear uppermost in her mind. She crept that way and stood where she could see through the window. She frowned before her face cleared and she headed to unlock the door.

The couple standing there grinned at Triese before greeting her. The two little toddlers also reached for hugs, chattering away without Triese being able to understand them.

"Brandon? Hagen? I wasn't expecting you today. Come in. And these are Heath and Hannah?" She stooped to hug the twins again, finding her face smothered in kisses. Hannah would not be outdone by her brother.

"That would be them." Brandon reached for Heath as Hannah simply climbed up Triese to be held, much to the dismay of her brother. Neither one liked the other to have something or to be held by someone if the other couldn't.

Hagen stood for a moment, her eyes on Triese She could see the strain that the younger lady was under. She could understand to a certain extent the fear and worry and stress that Triese was undergoing. She and Brandon had been through that.

"Come on into the kitchen. I had just put on a fresh pot of coffee and Teeg's mom sent cookies home with me yesterday." Triese had to stop talking because of the fierce hug she received from Hannah. "Do you like cookies?"

Hannah enthusiastically nodded as did Heath. They both struggled to get down and then ran for where they thought the kitchen would be. Both Hagen and Brandon looked mortified at the actions of their twins.

Triese could do nothing but laugh before she headed that way, her laughter lingering behind her. Hagen and Brandon shared a look before Hagen headed that way as well. Brandon took the opportunity to step outside and search. He wasn't into security, being in social work, but he knew enough of what to look for. Having had so many friends go through adventures as they called them, he was well aware that even the tiniest of objects could be a clue. And that was exactly what he did find.

Turning as he heard footsteps, Brandon stood with his feet planted on the driveway and his hands in his pockets. He frowned at the two men who were approaching before he saw Tait following them. One of the two men had to be Teeg and he was sure that the other was Toby. That man had the look of an officer about him. That was not something that could be hidden very easily.

"Brandon?" Tait reached to shake his friend's hand. "You're here. Your family as well?"

"We're all here. The twins are browbeating Triese though she seems to be able to handle them."

Tait laughed at the picture. He then pointed to Teeg and Toby.

"This is Teeg, Triese's fellow. And his brother, Toby. He's the investigator on the case." Tait watched the three men closely before he looked around. "Can we head inside? Someone is out here."

"There is." Brandon pointed towards the garage. "Toby, can you look into this?"

Toby nodded, heading for the garage with Brandon as the other two men headed for the house. Teeg hesitated for a moment, hearing laughter. He frowned. He didn't think that he had heard Triese laughing that freely.

Tait grinned. He was hearing the happy Triese that he had grown up with. He saw the look of wonder on Teeg's face and tapped him on the shoulder.

"This is Triese, Teeg. This is how she is when she's not under stress." He grinned once more and then headed for the kitchen.

Triese looked around and then headed for the hallway, finding Teeg still standing there, a look of wonder still evident on his face. She walked into his arms for his hug and then began to laugh as she felt a little body shoving inbetween them.

"No. No hug. Tre's mine." Heath stood there, his lower lip extended as he frowned at Teeg. He was not frightened off at all by Teeg's height.

Triese broke out into laughter once more as she scooped Heath up into her arms and dropped a kiss on his cheek.

"This is my guy, Heath. He'll share me with you but you have to share with Teeg. Okay?"

Heath frowned at her, the lower lip quivering for a moment.

"Still mine?" Heath almost strangled Triese with his tight hug. He turned in her arms, frowning at Teeg. He must have decided that he would share as he threw himself at the man. Teeg caught him and found himself covered in kisses and tight hugs.

Hagen had appeared, horror on her face once more as she watched her son.

"It's okay. You're Hagen? And this must be your son, Heath?" Teeg looked down as he felt a tug on the bottom of his T-shirt. "And you're Hannah?"

Hannah nodded emphatically and then scaled Teeg's tall frame to join her brother in showering Teeg with hugs and kisses. Teeg was laughing almost too hard to hold the two toddlers. He watched the light on Triese's face, once more taken with her beauty. His attention then went to Hagen, seeing her dismay at how her children were acting. He shook his head as she reached for Hannah.

"It's okay. I don't mind. Their joy is something that we need at this time. Thank you for coming, Hagen."

Chapter 32

Brandon and Toby walked in on Teeg's interaction with the toddlers. Brandon shared his wife's dismay. They were working with the strong-willed children. He was, however, unable to control his smile as he watched them, his eyes lighting on Hagen's face and then on Triese's. He frowned for a moment. There was something off today with her but he wasn't sure what. It had been that long since he had seen her.

Toby slapped his brother on his shoulder as he passed him, causing Heath to frown at him. A gentle hand rested against Heath's head before he hugged Triese and moved past her to the kitchen.

"Triese?" Brandon spoke at last, bringing her attention to him. "Are you okay?"

Triese moved past him to stand on the front porch, frowning at Roger before she stomped down the steps and stood nearby. Brandon followed her, watching the area around her for any signs of danger.

"Roger? What are you doing back here?" Triese moved closer to him before Brandon drew her back a ways. "Brandon? I want to know what's going on. It's my home that Roger is working on."

"We know that, Triese. Let him work. Toby wants to speak with you. In fact, he needs to." Brandon drew her back into the house despite her protests of not wanting to leave from where Roger was working."

"Brandon? What is going on out there?" Her finger stabbed towards the outdoors even as she tried to move around him and go back to watch Roger. She glared at him as he stood with his back against the door. She spun, intending to head for the back door and circle the house. Instead, she stopped abruptly, finding Toby waiting for her, a slightly amused look on his face.

"Triese? We do need to talk." His hand drew her away from the entryway and to her office. He watched with amusement still lurking in his eyes as she paced away from him.

"What did you find out there, Toby?" She refused to look at him.

"What did we find? Let's just say whatever it was? It is nasty. There was a dead squirrel tacked to the frame of the door. No note or anything to tell us who left it." Toby sobered as he spoke. "Did you hear anything over night?"

Triese stared at him in horror.

"A dead squirrel?" She stepped backwards, a hand to her mouth to try and control her emotions. "What is the meaning of that? And no, I didn't hear anything. And the security system did not alert. At least, I don't think that it did." She was at her computer, searching the security feed. "Nothing. And for them to come to the house, there should be. How did they do it?"

"That is something I would very much like to know. We'll be canvasing your neighbours to see if anyone heard or saw something." Toby smiled in sympathy as her face crumpled for a moment as she struggled to control her emotions. "We'll find them, Triese. Make no doubt about that. We will find them."

"I know that you will. But which one of us dies before you do that? And how do we even know that it is related to Tait or myself? Could someone be trying to exact revenge on someone who is close to us that we aren't aware of?" Triese brushed past him, a hand swiping at the tears on her face. She stopped abruptly as Teeg appeared and simply hugged her to him.

Toby walked past them and out of the front door to find Roger waiting for him. The distaste and dismay on Roger's face paused his steps.

"Roger?"

"There was a note, Toby. It was wrapped in plastic and stuffed in the squirrel's mouth. It threatens Triese with death unless she cooperates with them. What is she supposed to be cooperating about?" He handed over the evidence bag.

Toby, as hardened as he was to crime scenes, was taken aback by Roger's words. He shook his head as he read the note.

"I have no idea, and neither does she. And I need to speak with Tait." Toby handed the bag back to Roger before he walked away. He sat in his car, staring at the house, confused as to what was happening. No one seemed to know. That frightened him and not much did any more. But it was his brother and his lady as well has her brother that were being threatened. He could not solve this case without that one piece of missing information.

Pulling out his phone, Toby squinted at the text message. Brit needed to see him. Where could she find him? He sent a quick text, just stating that he was heading her way and would be there shortly.

Brit was pacing outside of her home, her eyes searching for Toby's car. She clutched the letter tightly in her hand, afraid for her brothers. Both had been threatened. And she didn't know which one to run to. Toby appeared in her vision, reaching to hug his sister and then to gently remove the paper from her hand.

"What is this, Brit?" Toby was deeply concerned. He didn't know if he had ever seen his sister so agitated.

"A threat, Toby. At threat at you and Teeg. Who wants to kill you?" Brit hugged her brother tighter before she moved back from him.

"Kill us? I have no idea." Toby uncrumpled the letter and read it. He drew in a deep breath. Brit was correct. Someone wanted Teeg and him dead. He just didn't know who or why. That was frustrating him beyond belief. And all he could do was cling to the promises of God being their shield and protector.

"They're watching all of us, Brit. How safe is your home?"

Brit shrugged. She had kept tightening her security over and over but still someone seemed to be able to get to her mailbox without being noticed.

"How are they getting to us, Toby? I spoke with Teeg while you were heading this way. He told me about the letter that Triese received."

"He did? And we have no idea who did what they did. It was gruesome, Brit. I am glad that Triese didn't see it."

"She's a lot stronger than you give her credit for. She has been in places where I wouldn't go, just to get the photos that she needed. A lot of dangerous places." Brit turned in a circle, not sure what to think or do. "So, Toby? How do we keep both you and Teeg safe?"

Triese shrugged. She had no idea how to do that. That was Toby's responsibility, wasn't it? She turned as she felt an arm around her and Teeg just stood, not saying anything. He had no idea what to say any way.

Chapter 33

Exhausted, Triese moved through the grocery store the next morning. She had not slept the night before, jumping at every little sound. The gruesome parcel left at her home the day before disturbed her beyond belief. She had nowhere to turn and didn't feel as if she had anyone that she could turn to. Triese knew that was incorrect but it was how she felt. She had finally sent Teeg home late the night before. He had not wanted to go but had reluctantly taken his leave.

Pausing with her hand reaching out for some apples, Triese frowned. She turned slightly to find a man watching her. She blinked and he was gone. Her blink had not been long enough for him to walk away. Instead, she looked up and breathed a thank you to her Heavenly Father. Her angel shield was there and would intervene if given permission by God.

Teeg appeared at her side, startling her.

"Teeg? What are you doing here?" She glared as he laughed at her surprise.

"The same thing that you are. I needed food. And it looks as if you did too. Care to shop together, darling?" Teeg continued to grin at her even as he felt the prickles beginning on his neck. Someone was watching him and he didn't like the threat that he felt.

Walking to their vehicles, Triese began to laugh. Somehow they had managed to park beside each other. Teeg grinned as well. His grin disappeared as he stared at the fluid collecting under her vehicle. His hand stopped her from approaching it before he was on his knees staring under it.

Triese was frustrated. She wanted to just put her groceries in her car and leave. Teeg was not letting her. Instead, he dropped her groceries into his truck along with his own. His hand on her arm drew her away despite her protests.

"Teeg? What are you doing? Let me go!" Her words were hissed at him.

"You're not getting into that car, Triese. The brake lines have been cut." Teeg shoved her onto a park bench and then pulled out his phone. He was growing very tired of having things like this happening and then having to call Toby to come to his rescue.

Triese frowned at him, anger radiating from her. She jumped to her feet and almost ran from him. Teeg stared after her, unable to follow at Toby answered his call.

Brit had been watching her brother and then was dismayed to see Triese running from him. She ran after Triese, the sound of her footsteps causing more fear in Triese.

"Triese? Wait up!" Brit's voice carried forward to Triese.

Triese drew in a deep breath. It was a friend who was calling out to her. She slid to a stop, turning as Brit approached her.

"Triese? Why are you running away? What did Teeg do to you?" Brit was concerned and almost frightened at the sight of her friend.

"Teeg didn't do anything. At least, I don't think that he did. He just took my groceries, dumped them in his truck, and rushed me away from my car. He told me that I couldn't drive it. And I have no idea why." Triese tromped back towards Teeg, Brit keeping pace with her. "Teeg? Why can't I drive my car?"

Teeg stared at her, his phone still in his hand. Toby was on his way and was sending Roger as well. He was tired of this and just wanted it all over. Only it didn't seem like it ever would be.

"Triese? Your car? The brake lines were cut. You can't drive it." Teeg shared a look with Brit, neither one of them ready for the storm that would be sure to follow. Or at least they thought that.

Triese sank down onto the park bench, a hand on her cheek as she stared towards her car. Why was this happening to her? She had no enemies. She didn't know who had kept Tait from his family for that long. And she certainly had no idea why Teeg was involved.

"Teeg? Who did this? Can't they just leave me alone? I don't need this. I'm supposed to travel next week and now I won't be able to. They're affecting my work." Triese was almost in tears. Brit sat beside her with an arm around her friend, watching her brother as he paced in front of them. Passersby sent quick glimpses their way before moving on.

Toby stood and watched as Roger worked away on the scene. This was something that he should have anticipated and had not. Why that was, he had no idea. He turned to look towards where the trio were waiting for him.

"Toby? They did a good job on them. She's going to have to have every brake line replaced. And there is no evidence that I can see. I'll grab the line when they remove them and see what I can determine. Has she called a tow truck yet?"

Toby shrugged. He had no idea if she had or not.

"Call ours and have it towed to our garage. I want you on this. Then have the mechanic replace her lines. She's family, whether she realizes it or not. All our people are trying to solve this."

"And no one has been able to, not yet." Roger was frustrated as well. He walked away to make the calls that he needed to, turning to watch as Toby trudged towards the three, his shoulders slumping in discouragement.

"Triese, did you have any problems with your brakes as you drove here?"

Triese shook her head. She hadn't noticed anything. But then again, she was not really alert to what was happening. She had been too lost in thought to notice.

"I can't tell you. I don't think so." Triese dropped her head, her hair brushing against her cheeks. She could hear the traffic in the parking lot and more faintly on the streets surrounding the area. She felt Teeg's arm tighten around her and then Brit's hand on hers. She looked up at Toby, seeing the stern look on his face. "Who is doing this, Toby? And why? Can you tell me that? I am tired of living like this, looking over my shoulder, searching every face that I pass just in case I need to remember them. Can you tell me that?" She was angry and almost spit the words at Toby. The three siblings stared at her. They had not seen this side of Triese.

Tait had approached them, having the same idea as his sister, needing to shop. He hesitated to approach before Toby waved him over.

"Tait? Your sister's brake lines have been slashed. Do you know anyone who would do that?" Toby's words were almost staccato as he uttered them.

Tait's eyes were on his sister even as his brain took in Toby's words. He paled, thinking of what could have happened. Triese was on her feet and hugging her brother. She didn't want her parents to know but she knew that at some point they would.

"Tait? Is this related to your work or to mine? Or are we off base with this?" Triese paced in the little area that she was allowed to. Her mind was now thinking in a more concise and uncluttered manner. "Teeg? Who would go after you?"

Teeg shrugged. He had tried to think of someone but he frowned as he studied his lady.

"Okay, so we think this through. Your work is with animals. Who would want you framed or removed from that area? And why?" Triese was trying to think through anything that could be the answer. She paced back to stand in front of Teeg.

"Poaching?" Tait was hesitant to say that but he felt that he had no choice. "What animals do you follow out there, Teeg, that could be poached?"

Teeg paled at Tait's words. It was a possibility that he had briefly consider and then set aside. Perhaps this was the reason after all. It just didn't explain Tait and Triese's involvement in that.

Chapter 34

The five stared at one another. Had Tait just uttered the reason for what was happening? It was entirely possible, they knew, but that didn't connect the siblings and Teeg.

"I did find evidence of poaching a few years ago. I've been watching since then but have not really noticed anything." Teeg turned to Tait. "Exactly when did you disappear?"

Tait stared at him, his mouth opening and closing. He was unable to speak for a moment.

"Two years ago this month. The men appeared and took me away. I had no chance to react or resist." Tait frowned as he remembered that.

Teeg's eyes slid closed. Tait had disappeared the same month as he found the bear carcasses with organs removed and the rest of the bear left to whichever animal would feast upon it. He turned to Triese, finding her watching her brother closely.

"Triese? Where were you taking photos at that time?" Teeg waited patiently for Triese to respond.

Triese stared at Teeg and then at her brother. Her face paled before she staggered sideways and then slumped onto the bench. She knew exactly where she had been and what she had been taking photos of. That had become crystal clear as they had gone over the photos over the past week or so.

"I was here. I was taking photos out near Teeg's place. On the side of the creek where Teeg found me. A client asked for photos of certain animals, including bears. It took me a few days to get what he wanted." She looked up, a devastated look on her face. "Is he the one? Is he behind this?"

Toby crouched down beside her, an arm resting on the arm of the bench. He wanted the pedestrians moving through the parking lot, the traffic that moved slowly, and then focused on Roger and the tow truck for the police department. He sighed to himself.

"Who is it, Triese? I need to know that. And then we'll need the photos from that time frame." Toby continued to wait, not sure if she would even respond.

"I don't know if his name is correct now." She uttered a name, causing Toby to frown and then look up at Teeg.

Teeg was troubled as he watched Triese. He took Brit's place beside her and wrapped her in his arms. He knew the man and had had interactions with him. Those interactions had been violent in words from the man and threatening as well. Teeg had walked away from the last interaction, determined to have no further contact with that man. Now, however, it seems that he was under attack once more from him.

"I didn't know." Triese blinked back tears. "How was I to know?" She swiped at her tears. "How do we do this? I need to go back over those photos." She stared at Toby as he shook his head.

“Let me have copies of them. I’ll have the lab techs go over them. It’s the proper way to do it.” Toby was on his feet, heading for Roger who had approached him.

“We’ll get your photos to Toby. Let’s head that way and find them.” Teeg drew Triese to her feet and headed for his truck. Brit paced beside them. She had walked to the store that day but for now, she wanted to be with her brother and his lady.

Triese scrambled through the photos, trying to find the ones that she needed. She handed them to Teeg as he stood waiting. Brit was tight to his side to study them. Her finger pointed to one photo.

“Who’s that?” Brit’s keen eyes had spotted someone hiding in the trees, watching towards the camera.

“That’s him.” Teeg sighed, fear moving through his heart.

“Who?” Triese was on her feet, her hand reaching to tilt Teeg’s. “Is that him? I didn’t ever see him in person. A lot of my contacts and requests are done over the internet. That’s how it was with him. He was stalking me at that point.” Triese frowned at the date. “That’s the day that Tait disappeared. He was watching me to find out when I knew, wasn’t he? He planned this. He had me out of range of any cell service.” Triese was growing angry. That anger she knew had to be given to God. She just wasn’t ready to do that.

“It is?” Brit paced away, her phone out to call Toby. “Toby? Triese has a picture of the man watching her. The thing is that photo was taken on the day that Tait disappeared. Triese was not where she had any cell service."

"It was planned, then." Toby walked rapidly towards his car, sliding inside, and then just sitting there. "She has a photo of him. That was careless." He knew then that's why Triese had been targeted, at least in part. And Teeg? He was certain that Tait was correct, that poachers were after Teeg to destroy him. Fear grew within Toby's heart. "I'll head your way. You're at Triese's?"

"We are. Hurry, Toby. I really don't like this." Brit tucked her phone away, glancing at the clock. "Hey, guys. I have to leave. I have a meeting."

Teeg nodded, not looking at his sister. Brit gave a grim smile before she walked away, heading for her home. It really wasn't that far away. She didn't see the car that had parked across the street from Triese's home, the two men inside watching her leave before their attention went back to the house.

"Triese? Talk to me." Teeg wrapped her into his arms. "I'm here for you, darling. This doesn't change how I feel about you. I do love you."

Triese nodded, her attention turned to Teeg. She looked up at him, seeing the love that he had for her on his face.

"I love you, too." Triese hugged him. "What do we do now?"

"Toby is on his way to find that photo. Do you have all of them from that date?" Teeg didn't want to let her go.

"I do. They're in that folder. How did I ever not see him?" Triese was suddenly terrified and that made her cling harder to Teeg. He made her feel safe. In Triese's mind, he was the soldier holding a shield in front of them. She was just afraid that he would die and she would lose the love that God had provided for her.

Chapter 35

Toby walked towards Triese's house, pausing as he saw the open front door. That was not normal for her, he knew, especially at this time. He reached for his weapon, clasping it in both hands, as he approached the house, calling out for Triese. When he received no answer, he searched the house and then the yards, not finding any sign of Triese or Teeg.

Worried about his brother, Toby ran for his car and called for help. They would need to search the neighbourhood but his gut feeling was that his brother had disappeared as had Triese. He frowned as he saw Tait's car parked beside Teeg's truck. That meant that Tait had disappeared as well.

Tyler approached his nephew, worry on his face.

"Toby? What can you tell me?" Tyler paused in the entryway, watching as officers searched the home.

"Not a lot. Triese had photos for me that showed the man who we think is responsible for what is going on." Toby mentioned the name, causing Tyler to pause and then Tyler's face paled.

"Him? He's ruthless in his dealings. So far, we have never had any evidence that he has crossed the legal line."

"No, we don't. I have Anna working on that right now." He held up a folder that had a sticky note with his name on it. "Triese left this for me. I know that I need to go through these photos. I'll have the lab do that first."

"Sounds about right. Now, what can you tell me about this?" Tyler's hand waved towards the interior of the house.

"Not a lot, unfortunately. They just seem to have walked out of the house. I don't like it, Uncle Ty."

"None of us do. We want to find them but we don't know what happened. What about her security feed?" Tyler looked towards the control panel on the wall.

"It's been tampered with. It's of no help. Brit left about thirty minutes ago. Tait must have arrived shortly after. I talked to Brit. She didn't see anything out of the ordinary." Toby was frustrated at Teeg and Triese disappearing once more. They still did not have a good handle on why or a confirmed presence behind them.

Toby dropped his jacket over his desk chair late that afternoon. He had been on the run for the whole day and desperately needed something to eat and a coffee. Sitting, he reached for the bag of fast food before his head dropped to pray. He was begging God to bring his brother home safely. He kept his head bowed for a moment until he felt somewhat at peace.

Reaching for the folder of photos, Toby slowly opened it, knowing that he might find some of the answers that he was searching for. He went over each photo carefully, making his notes. He paused at the photo that showed the man. Toby studied him and then stood to pace. Why was that man there? How deep was he involved in this? Leaving his office, he stalked towards Anna's office, hoping that she might have answers. Only, she wasn't there. She was out on a crime scene.

At a loss, Toby hesitated before he returned to his office, grabbed his jacket, and locked the door. He walked away, not sure where he was heading but knowing that he had to do something. Just what that something was, he didn't know. He finally headed for his parents, knowing that they would be highly worried about Teeg.

Titus hugged his son before they moved back into the house. Toby could hear voices and looked with a question at his father.

"Your mom. Brit. Triese and Tait's parents. Roger. Tyler. Ed. And Anna is on her way." Titus gave a tight grin. "But first, son. Talk to me. Tell me how you are." His concerned eyes watched his son closely.

Toby shrugged. At the moment, he had no idea how he felt. He was too deep into worry for his brother to even act as a police officer and investigator at that point. He knew that he would get back to his work mode but for now, he was a hurting brother.

"I don't know, Dad. I really don't know. I didn't expect Teeg to disappear again." Toby leaned against the wall, sorrow in his gaze. "How do we find him and the others?" His hand went up at his father went to speak. "The force will do that. I was just thinking out loud."

"And well you should be. Now, we'll eat as best we can and then spend time in prayer. After that, Brandon is on his way with Dallas and they'll work with us. Sometimes, civilians work better to find people."

"I know, Dad. I know that. I just didn't expect it to be this." Toby was repeating himself without realizing it.

Titus watched his son, seeing the worry and distress that he was trying hard to hide.

"Don't hide your worry from us, son." Titus directed his son towards the kitchen with a hand on his shoulder. "We're all hurting, Toby. Together, we'll figure it all out." Titus turned as he heard a tap at the door, opening it to find Brandon and Dallas. "You're early, fellows. Have you eaten?"

"No, but it's okay." Dallas didn't want to put the family to any more work than was necessary.

"We're doing some grilling. Hamburgs. And there is plenty. We'll eat and then pray." Titus watched the two men move that way before he turned and stepped outside. He looked up at the darkening sky, begging God for his son and his son's lady and her brother. Tyler stopped beside him, an arm across his brother's shoulders.

"Tyler? What are the odds of them coming home safe and sound?" Titus was almost afraid to ask.

Tyler shrugged. He didn't know and didn't want to raise Titus' hopes.

"I can't give those odds, Titus. It's not possible. All we can do is search for them and pray that God protects them and shields them from harm. We also have to be prepared for the worst case scenario. And that is very hard to do." Tyler's arm tightened on his brother's shoulders as Titus struggled with his emotions.

"That's the hard part, Ty. It's the part where they might never be found or if they're found, we have to bury them. Even if they come back safe, they will never be the same. Not after all this. Triese said that she could see the change in Tait with his captivity."

"And it will change them. We can't prevent that. All we can do is surround them with prayer, no matter where they are." Tyler's head turned slightly as he heard the door open and Timothy appeared. "Timothy?"

"It's okay, Tyler. I wondered where you two were. I'll leave as I'm interrupting." He stopped as Titus' hand landed on his shoulder.

"You're not interrupting, Timothy. If anything, it's worse, much worse, for you. You have two children missing. I only have one. And once more, you are facing the uncertainty of knowing where they are and if they are safe."

Timothy nodded, a sober look on his face. He stood for a moment, lost in thought, his eyes on the stars and moon that were just now peeking out from the clouds. He could hear the night sounds of nature around him.

"It is worse for me but it's still as bad for you. We don't know where our children are or even if they are alive. God is in control. It's hard, sometimes, to let go and let Him lead."

Chapter 36

Two days had gone by since the trio had disappeared. No amount of searching had found them. Their families were not sleeping and exhaustion was slowing down their responses.

Toby had managed to grab some sleep, a couple of hours at a time. He felt overwhelmed with the number of investigations that were cropping up. All of the investigators felt that way and they could not understand it. Toby was of a mind that someone was behind all this and that one person was the one who had kidnapped his brother and the two siblings.

Heading into the detachment, Toby paused for a moment. He shook his head as a thought crossed his mind. What if this man was just the front man and someone else was behind it? That stopped him in his tracks and sent him almost running for his office to start that investigation.

Tyler paused outside of the conference room, watching as Toby and Anna worked away inside. He heard footsteps stop beside and looked that way. Roger stood beside him, papers in his hands.

"Roger?" Tyler waited patiently for Roger to speak.

"Tyler?" Roger held up the papers. "This. Toby was right. He thought that there was someone behind that man. This proves it. It also gives the multiple names and addresses that he uses."

"Who is it?" Tyler's face hardened as he heard the name. It was not who he had expected. "Okay. In with you. Tell Toby to find me when he has all the confirmation that he needs. We'll move in with the warrants when he's ready to."

"I'll tell him but I'm sure he knows that." Roger walked into the room, heading for Toby.

Toby took the papers and listened as Roger explained what he had discovered. He was not surprised. He had always had a suspicion about that man.

"What about his family?" Toby searched through the paperwork. "I don't see that you have found anything on them."

"I'm still running information. About Triese's car? We have been looking through the videos at the store. I don't see that it was tampered with there. That means that someone was at her home and did it. And I have her security feed. Her father let me in to get it. I don't see anyone moving around but it was heavily clouded that night before Teeg found the fluid."

"And that would help to hide anyone moving in." Tyler was frustrated at that. "Okay, keep working on what you have. The letters?"

"Computer printed with nothing to help identify whoever left them." Roger was frustrated at that. "I'll work on this as I can. What's with all that evidence from all those crime scenes?"

Toby nodded absentmindedly. He had no idea what was going on with that and didn't suspect that he would ever know.

Toby stretched at last as he rose from the chair that he had been sitting in for hours. He looked around. He was the only one left, the others have moved on to other tasks or left for the night. Toby squinted at his watch and sighed. He needed to get out of there but he was still looking for that one piece of information that he could not find. He knew himself well enough that he needed to walk away from the investigation for a day.

The next morning, Toby walked his brother's property. He had arrived that morning to find Andy wanting to run for the forest. He had approached his brother's cabin the day he disappeared to find Andy frantic inside the building.

Andy had been shut in for hours, pacing the rooms and actively searching for a way out. He had jumped up at each window and found them closed. If they had been open only a little bit, Toby knew that Andy would have pushed at the window until he had it open enough to get out and then he would have just gone through the screen. Whoever had locked Andy in had ensured that the windows were closed. Toby knew that Teeg would have left the windows open a few inches due to the heat that day.

Walking in step with Toby, Andy searched the area around the cabin. He was not alerting to anything or that anyone had been around that day. Toby had prayed that he would find evidence that Teeg or Triese or even Tait had been there. He had not found that evidence. He was saddened by that and watched as Andy's demeanour had changed.

Andy was missing Teeg, Toby could tell. He called the dog to where he had seated himself on the steps to the porch and hugged him to him.

"You're missing him, aren't you, boy? So am I. Where are we going to find him?" Toby sat for a while before he was on his feet and then walking around the house. He didn't think that he would find anything and he was correct. He headed for his truck that he had parked near the garage. Toby had often asked Teeg why he didn't build a garage closer to cabin. Teeg had shrugged and simply stated that he agreed with the previous owner. Not having a vehicle near the cabin let the animal and bird and insect population not to be chased away. Besides, being that close to the road meant that he didn't have a long driveway to shovel when winter sent heavy snow. Toby had not thought of that but he agreed with his brother.

Stopping to stare at the garage, Toby moved that way and searched around it. There was nothing there that he could see. Andy was not alerting to anything either and Toby knew the dog well enough to know that he would if he found anything off. He allowed Andy into the truck and then just sat behind the wheel, lost in thought. He wondered where his brother was and if he was all right. He had no way of knowing that.

Driving away, Toby did not see the man who had stepped from the shadows of the garage to watch him. The man nodded. He would find some way to reach out to Toby. He knew where the trio were being held and they needed Toby's help urgently. He had just been too late to stop Toby from driving away.

Andy stood from where he had been curled up on the front seat to look through the back window. He began to bark, startling Toby who pulled his truck to the side of the road. He shifted to stare behind him, movement near the garage catching his attention. He spun his wheel and headed back that way, intent on what was in front of him.

Slamming his door behind him which was something he never did, Toby ran for the garage, Andy racing ahead of him. Toby slid to a stop as he saw the man standing there.

"Where did you come from? You weren't here five minutes ago." Toby's hand was resting on his weapon.

"No need for the weapon, Toby. I was hoping to catch you and thought that I had missed you. My name is John." John held up a hand as he saw the frown on Toby's face. "I know where your brother is. If you come with me, we can find him and the others and release them." John looked past him. "And you have friends here to help."

"I do?" Toby spun to see Brandon and Dallas emerging from Brandon's truck and then Richard and his team of four appearing. "What are you doing here?"

"God." Brandon's reply was terse. "God told us to be here. And it looks as if we're where we're supposed to be."

Chapter 37

The group stared at one another and then at John. It seemed as if he was the one in the know, as they say, as to where the three would be found. Naomi frowned as she studied him, sensing that he was not who he seemed to be. John caught her look and gave a slight shake of his head. She sighed. She needed to talk to Richard but there was no way that she could at the moment. She suspected that Triese was correct in her suppositions. There was an angel on earth looking out for them.

John studied the six men and two ladies. They needed to move out and move out quickly. He was well aware of who they all were and how they would be able to handle the trek.

"John? What can you tell us?" Toby spoke for the group, knowing that he had to. He was in charge of the investigation and needed to be the lead in this.

"I know where they are. It's a couple of hours from here. Do you have gear with you or do you need to find some?"

"We're all set." Richard spoke for his group, seeing Brandon and Dallas nodding. He studied Dallas, surprised to see him. An investigator who had retired to take on a new role with the Barnabas Foundation, Dallas was around their own age. He too had had an adventure with his now wife, Deri.

"I can grab what I need from Teeg's cabin. Let's move. And Andy comes with us." Toby moved over,

Andy pacing at his side, and quickly grabbed what he needed for both himself and Andy. Andy had waited patiently for Toby to change his collar to the one he recognized as his search and rescue collar. Toby watched the dog's demeanour change from being a pet to being a working dog. He trusted Andy, having worked with him and Teeg on search missions.

John studied each member of the group. He trusted them, he decided, knowing that they would work together to find the trio and get them to safety. John was afraid of the danger that they were facing but knew that it was nothing new for them, not even for Brandon who was not in law enforcement.

"Okay, John, before we move out, we pray." Toby was adamant about that. He watched as John nodded.

"Of course we do. We can't move forward unless we do." John bowed his head to lead off in prayer followed by each one of the group. All prayed for protection and that God would be the shield that was needed for their friends.

John led the way, heading for Willow Creek and then crossing the log that Teeg had carried Triese across all those days ago. He paused for a moment before he pointed ahead.

"That way. We should have enough light to get us there." He strode off, leaving the others behind him to share a look before they walked forward. It was not the first time that they had headed out. There was little conversation between them. Andy surged ahead at times, seeming to sense that he was heading towards

Teeg. There was no way that Toby was going to let him loose. Andy would just take off and head for where he thought Teeg was.

Two hours later, John held up his hand. He waited patiently for the group to come to a halt, their eyes on him. He motioned for them to be quiet and then pointed at Toby and Richard and motioned for them to follow him. They crept forward, hands out to hold branches away from their faces. Their feet were placed carefully on the twigs and leaves as they tried their best not to make any noise.

John halted them again just before they entered the clearing ahead of them. He looked around and then pointed. The two men looked at him and then peered through the dusk. Toby drew in a deep breath as he saw the three bodies. His first instinct was to charge forward. Richard's hand on his shoulder kept him in his place.

Toby stared around, not seeing any guards. He leaned closer to John.

"Where are the guards?" His voice was kept to a low whisper. He could see Richard studying the area and knew that he was running scenarios on how to get in and out quickly.

"They haven't been here, I don't think, all day." John hesitated to continue. "They were left here to die, you know."

Toby had already come to that conclusion. It scared him, he had to admit.

"How do we do this?"

“Richard, you and your team go in. Dallas and Toby go with you.” He handed over bolt cutters, startling the two men with him. “You’ll need these.” John disappeared to bring the others waiting out of sight forward. “You’re in charge, Richard. Your team knows best how to get in and out. Toby? Dallas?”

“We’re with them. We’ll collect what evidence we can.” Toby moved forward with Dallas at his side. He slid to a stop, horrified as he saw the three. “They’re shackled to the trees! How long have they been here?”

“At least a day, I would suspect.” Richard moved forward, working the bolt cutters to release the trio. He watched as Toby and Dallas worked to collect what evidence there was. He turned to watch Stephen, the paramedic on his team, do a quick assessment of the three.

Teeg was stretched out on his back, a hand on his chest. He didn’t respond to the hands on him. Stephen moved to Triese, who was curled up on her side, an arm tucked under her head. She too did not respond to Stephen. His attention then turned to Tait. Tait was stretched out on his abdomen. His head raised slightly as Stephen’s hand touched his back. He just shook his head at the questions that were fired at him before his head was back on his outstretched arm.

Richard walked to where Stephen had risen to his feet and was watching the three.

“Stephen? Talk to me.” Richard knew that Stephen would have a good idea of how the three were.

"Richard? We need to get them out of here. It's getting dark and it's a long trek. As to their conditions? Teeg and Triese have not responded. Tait roused but not fully enough to get a clear answer." Stephen watched as Toby moved to his brother as he was raised to his feet, positioning himself to drape Teeg over his shoulders. Brandon had moved in to do the same with Tait. Dallas had gathered Triese into his arms. The three then headed towards where John was standing. "Who is John?"

"I have no idea, Stephen. Head off. I'll take the rear. Naomi and Silver are in front. Keep an eye on the three. If we need to stop, we'll do that."

Richard eyed the cleaning, not seeing anything that would lead to who had chained and shackled the trio in that clearing. He was puzzled as to why and who. He looked up, seeking for answers and not finding any.

Chapter 38

Following John back towards Teeg's cabin, the group made their way through the dark. Andy refused to leave Toby's side, his head turning up to watch his master. Low whines emanated from him, so low that only Toby could hear him. His whispered words to the dog didn't really help relieve Andy's distress.

Afterwards, the group had stared at each other. They had walked back to Teeg's cabin as if they were walking in the sunlight. Yet, they knew that it was pitch black. None of them could explain it afterwards and talked about it softly among themselves.

Sorting out who would ride in what vehicle, Toby stood beside Richard and watched as the trio were carefully placed, one to a vehicle. He had insisted that Teeg was in his. Tait was with Brandon and Dallas. Triese ended up in Richard's truck, Silver and Naomi on either side of her. Toby's hand reached for Andy, knowing that he should leave the dog behind but he didn't have the heart to. He would use the search and rescue card if he had to just to make sure that Andy was with Teeg. He somehow didn't think that he would need to.

Richard turned in a circle, a frown on his face. He was searching for John and not finding him.

"Toby? Where's John?"

"John?" Toby spun in a circle, not finding the man. He paused before he looked up, a quiet thank you whispered to his Heavenly Father. "John? I think that he's the angel that Triese has talked about. He's not here. How did he just appear and just disappear as he did? It has to be God."

"She's adamant about that?" Richard shook his head and then paced to his truck, ready to head for Red Oak and medical help for the three.

Toby was out of his truck and through the ambulance bays and heading for the medical staff. They stared at him in shock before rushing for stretchers and then heading for the trio. Quickly assessed, the three were moved to stretchers and then rushed into examination rooms. Toby paced, Andy's leash tight in his hand. He paused before he reached for his phone. He called Tyler first.

"Uncle Ty?" He could tell that Tyler had been sleeping.

"Toby? What's going on?" Tyler paused before he spoke again. "You found them?"

"We did. They're here at the hospital right now."

"Good. I'm on my way. Have you called for guards?" Tyler was dressing rapidly, waiting for Toby to respond.

"Not yet. Richard and his team are here and are doing that. I'll call in some officers as well." Toby didn't quite know how to explain what happened.

"You can tell me when I get there." Tyler hung up on the call, taking a moment to breathe a prayer of thanks.

Toby turned away from the examination rooms, heading for the waiting room. He needed to call his parents. He knew that Brit would be there with them.

"Mom?" Toby knew that his mother had not retired as yet. She would have been in her prayer corner, begging God for the three to come home."

"Mom? Can you come?" Toby struggled with his tears. "To the hospital?"

"Toby? Have you been hurt?" Sari was on her feet, heading for the kitchen where Titus and Brit was trying to figure out the mystery. Timothy and Abygayle were there as well. They all looked at her as she appeared in the doorway.

"No, I'm fine, Mom. Teeg, Triese, and Tait are here." He continued to struggle with his emotions. He felt a hand on his shoulder as Dallas waited beside him.

"What?" Sari's forward walk stopped abruptly. Her eyes shot to Titus. "You have them? They're safe?" A sob caught at her throat as Titus wrapped her into his arms.

"We have them, Mom. They're unconscious right now and we have to do the interviews. But you need to come. I need to find Timothy and Abygayle." He looked around, at a loss for a moment.

"They're here, son. We'll be there shortly." Sari's phone was back in her pocket as she clung to her husband. "Titus? They're safe. Toby wants us to come."

"And we will. Let's pray first and then head that way. One vehicle will do." Titus was as good as his word, shepherding the others out to his car and then driving as fast as he could towards the hospital. He drew in a deep breath as he saw the emergency lights come on behind him and his foot lifted from the accelerator. He watched as the patrol vehicle pulled around him and then in front of him. He watched as an arm appeared outside of the vehicle and waved him to follow the officer. Titus' foot pressed down again as they raced across town.

Running inside, they first spotted Andy who was on his feet, whining as he saw them. Brandon had the leash by that point and just let go of it for Andy to run to Teeg's family. They could tell just how upset the dog was.

Toby spun as he heard the hurried footsteps and found himself wrapped in his mother's arms, his father's arms around the pair. Brit moved in on them. His eyes found those of Triese and Tait's parents.

"Mom, Dad? They're still working on them. I can't explain all what happened but someone led us to where they were. We brought them out." Toby couldn't and wouldn't say how they had been found. For now, it was enough that they were here and safe. He nodded at his uncle as he walked past him, headed for the examination rooms.

"They're okay?" Abygayle approached Toby, hugging him in turn. "What happened?"

"I was out at Teeg's. The others showed up. Someone was there who knew where they were. We went in, found them, and brought them out." Toby looked past his family to meet Dallas' eyes. That man nodded. They were in agreement that they would say nothing.

"There was? Okay. When can we see them?" Timothy found the ward clerk and then returned. "They're still working on them. How long does it take?"

Chapter 39

Toby paced towards Teeg's room, not sure if his brother would be awake or not. He needed him to wake up and tell him just what happened. Anna had headed for Triese and Tyler was with Tait. They needed to speak with the trio before the family appeared to be with them. He just wasn't sure that would happen.

Teeg had begun to stir, finding that he was warm once more and felt safe. His eyes cracked open before they closed. A tear trickled down his cheek as he realized that someone had indeed found him and had him safe. He prayed for Triese and Tait, begging God that would have brought them to safety as well. A hand on his shoulder caused him to jump before he looked up.

"Toby? Where are I?" Teeg had to clear his throat to get any words out. He sipped gratefully at the glass of water that Toby held to his lips.

"You're in our hospital, Teeg. What happened?" Toby looked around, not sure what to say. "Triese and Tait are safe." He could see the relief that Teeg felt.

"I don't really know." Teeg raised the head of the bed, his eyes closing briefly as his head spun. "How long?"

"How long? Two days at the most. What happened?" Toby asked again.

"I can't really remember. We were at Triese's. In her office. She had gone to find something for us to eat. We heard a noise and looked around to see Triese standing in the doorway. A man was standing behind her, his arm tight around her neck. Her head was shoved tight to his arm. She was terrified, Toby, and there was nothing that Tait or I could do for her. We were forced from the house. Triese had to lock it up as she usually did when she left. She resisted and that man slapped her across the face. We were too far away to help her even if we could have gotten away. By that time, our wrists were handcuffed in front of us.

"The four men shoved us into two trucks. There were already drivers behind the wheel. Tait and Triese were shoved in one and I was shoved into another one. We were taken to a home on the other side of Willow Creek. The men never said a word. We were then forced into a shed at the back of the house, each of us chained to a wall stud that was not close enough to one another to do anything or to reach one another. Tait was really quiet. I think that he recognized the men but he never said. I don't think that he wanted to. I am sure that they were listening for us to talk.

"Triese just withdrew. She wouldn't look at either one of us. I don't understand the why, Toby. Do you?" Teeg watched as Toby shook his head. "Any way, we were left there overnight with no water or food. The next morning, just as dawn was breaking, the men returned and made us leave the shed. We were walked for a couple of hours. Triese was having trouble keeping on her feet but the men would not let either Tait or I help her. She stumbled and fell a number of times. She was hurt, I think, a couple of times that she fell. I heard her cry out.

"They marched us to a clearing and then made us stop in the centre of it. Triese was pulled away from us and that's when their plans became very clear. She was shackled to a tree. I tried to reach her to prevent it but they knocked me out. I remember rousing every once in a while but not enough to know what was going on. What happened after that, Toby? Were Tait and I shackled to trees as well?"

"You were. Tait roused enough to tell us that. You had no water or food with you. And I can confirm that you were there for at least a day and a half. We found you early this evening." Toby shifted on the chair that he had drawn up to the bed. "Can you describe the men, Teeg?"

"I can." He reached for the notepad and the pen that Toby was reaching out to him. He scribbled away for a while. Exhausted, Teeg handed the notepad back to Toby. "Their names are there. We know them, Toby. We know them from church and from contact in town. Who is behind this?"

"We know who it is, Toby. We just can't say until we finalize the investigation. What you and Triese and Tait just went through just adds to that. We're working as best as we can." Toby was on his feet. "Mom, Dad, and Brit are waiting to see you. So is Andy. He's been allowed to stay." Toby walked away, not seeing the weary nod that Teeg gave.

Andy ran through the door, his leash dragging behind him. He was on the bed and nestled down as tight to Teeg as he could get, his tongue licking at Teeg's face. Titus, Sari, and Brit moved to stand around the bed, seeing that Teeg was almost asleep.

They hugged him and then Titus and Brit walked away, leaving Teeg's mother on guard for her son. She tucked the blankets up around him as much as she could, a hand resting on his hair before it rested against Andy. Andy was not leaving. They would have to physically drag him away to do that.

Timothy and Abygayle were torn. They could be with both of their children but who went to who. Timothy took his wife's hand and headed first for their daughter. They watched as she moved restlessly, not rousing at all to talk with them. Tait's room was next. Tait was awake but refused to say what happened. Tait was deeply afraid for his family. They had been threatened with death if he spoke at all. Tyler had managed to get a statement of sorts from him but that man knew that there was more that had happened.

Abygayle sent her husband back to their daughter, finding a chair to plant by Tait's bedside. He looked over at her, a frown on his face before he sighed. He knew that his mother would not leave him. It was how she was. He looked past her as Titus entered the room. He would not even speak with that man.

Toby tracked down Richard and pointed to the outside of the hospital. The men moved that way, Toby pausing to stare up at the sky. It was getting near to morning and he was exhausted. He would not leave yet but would have to do so at some time. He took with thanks the cup of coffee held out to him.

"Richard? What are your thoughts about this?" Toby was asking as a victim's brother, not as an officer this time.

“My thoughts? You’ve solved the case, haven’t you? This was an attempt to remove the witnesses from your investigation. If they were not here, you would have a hard time proving your case. The man that you are after is very careful.” He looked past Toby to see Dallas standing there. “Dallas?”

“I agree. This is a deliberate attempt at murder. Now, you need to prove it. That means you’ll be working around the clock to do so. Make sure that you do take breaks, Toby.” Dallas knew what he was saying, having been an investigator himself.

“I know, Dallas. I know. I want this over. This was just too close for them.” Toby was sober. “Do you realize that they had no water with them? Do you know what kind of death that would have been? And being out there and shackled as they were? They were out there in the open, at the mercy of any predator that would have approached them.”

Chapter 40

Triese curled up in a corner of the couch at Titus' home. She was wrapped in a blanket, not feeling safe as yet but feeling much warmer. She didn't want the feeling that she had had when they were left in the open. She had been terrified until she had lost consciousness. Teeg was at her side, his arm around her, tucking her tight to him.

Teeg didn't want to let go of his lady. He had been terrified that they would not survive what had happened to them. He watched as Tait snuggled down under a blanket in a nearby chair. He heard their parents speaking in the kitchen and knew that Toby, Brit, and Tyler were there. Richard and his team were outside, not willing to let them be on their own.

Toby approached the trio, assessing them. He sighed. They were acting as victims of crime, which they were. It would take time and counselling for them to get over it. He sat, knowing that he had to talk with them but was reluctant to do so. The investigation had been completed, but not how they would have wanted it to. He was on his feet to help his mother and Abygayle with the trays that they were carrying.

The meal completed and the debris and dishes cleared away, Titus shared a look with Timothy before his head was bowed and he began to pray. The prayer went through them all, drawing them all to God's throne. They acknowledged how He had been the shield and protector that the trio had needed.

Titus raised his head, searching the faces of his son and then the other two. They no longer had that look of innocence that they had. That disturbed and saddened him.

Toby looked around as well, finding Tyler watching him and then nodding. It was time for the investigation to be revealed to the group. He cleared his throat, preparatory to speaking. He frowned for a moment, a thought chasing through his mind. He just couldn't grasp the tail of it to stop it.

"Toby?" Teeg's voice broke the silence that was deepening. "What can you tell us? You've gone over what happened when you found us. But that doesn't explain why or who."

"No, it doesn't. You three were left to die there, you know. And we knew why now." Toby looked down for a moment. "The reason? You were preventing them from poaching more than they had been able to. You know the market out there for black market organs. The wilderness that you protect? There are so many animals that they wanted to kill and take the organs from. You prevented that. They felt that if they could rid of you, they would walk right in and take what they wanted.

"Triese? That photo with the man in it? You didn't realize that you had taken his photo. He tracked you down and has watched you for years. You didn't realize that. You have moved to this town to set up your photography business but he knew where you were from. Tait? You were taken because of that. Triese had the evidence to prove that he was involved and Teeg kept him from making profits from crime.

You were to be held until Triese and Teeg were dealt with. It took time for them to confirm what they needed to and then to make their plans. We have confirmed that many attempts had been made to do just that.

"Triese? The day that you disappeared? It was his men who took you and dropped you on that side of the creek. You had been sedated and they felt that being out overnight would be enough to kill you. They were surprised when it didn't work out. Teeg, it was part of their plan to accuse you of kidnapping Triese. That didn't work out either." Toby couldn't give all the details. Those would need to wait for trial.

"I was taken back then with this plan in place?" Tait was shocked, to say the least. "Who?" When Toby didn't respond, Tait spoke again, anger in his voice. "Who, Toby? Who took two years of my life away from me that I'll never see again."

"Who? It's not someone that you know, Tait. Edward Lynn is the name that we know him by." Toby could hear the rumours in the room as he said the name. He kept his eyes locked on Tait. "And he does have an alias. Leo Eden."

"Leo Eden?" Timothy's face paled. "He tried to get me to work for him but he really didn't seem to have a position for me. I often wondered if it was a fishing expedition. Now, it appears that it was."

"It was. He already had plans in place. Unfortunately, we can't ask him what they all were. He resisted arrest last night and was shot when he tried to kill an officer. He didn't make it." Toby was sober as he gave that information. He also went on to confirm that everything that they had gone through had been at Lynn's direction.

Toby rose at last, heading for his home. He was exhausted and had been ordered by his supervisor not to come in for a week. Tyler walked out with him. He gave his nephew a hug and sent him on his way. He watched as a patrol car moved out to follow Toby. Even though they had everyone under arrest, there was still a sense of uncertainty.

John stood in the shadows and watched Tyler before he slipped by him and into the house. He stood in the hallway watching those in the living room. Triese looked up at that point and saw him, a light of thanks on her face. Tait had been watching her and looked at John as well, a frown on his face as he tried to think of who he was. Teeg had watched as John had appeared. The three blinked and when they looked, John was gone. Teeg heard Triese's quiet words of John being an angel. He had to agree.

Tait thought back to what they had been told of how they had been returned to Teeg's cabin. He was well aware that it was night at the time. However, each one present had simply stated that the path was as clear as if it was daylight in front of them but dark behind them. Their only explanation was John.

Quiet grew in the living room before the parents moved to clear the kitchen and then find their rest. Tait rose too and headed for the room that he was to use.

Teeg was reluctant to let go of Triese and Triese was just as reluctant to leave him. She looked up at him to find his head lowering towards her as he kissed her. He then wrapped her tighter in his arms.

"Okay, darling?"

"I think so, Teeg. I still can't believe that we went through what we did and all for the sake of poaching. I didn't realize that it was so dangerous."

"It can be. God protected both of us and also served as a shield for Tait. Things could have gone bad so quickly."

"It could have." Triese yawned before she slept.

Teeg looked down at her before a hand rested on Andy's head. Andy had climbed up beside Teeg and was laying as close to his master as he could. Teeg looked up, thanking and praising God for being their shield and protector.

Epilogue

Six months later, Teeg straightened his tie as he watched Andy closely. Andy had a huge bow around his neck and was eager to find the lady who he wanted to protect so badly. Teeg laughed at him as he reached to ring the doorbell to Triese's house. He fingered the small box in his pocket.

Triese slid her hands down the skirt of her flowered dress. It hit her legs just at mid-calf. She was nervous that night and wasn't sure why. Teeg and she had been dating for months now. Tonight, Triese just sensed that something was about to change and she wasn't sure if she was ready for that.

Opening the door, Triese's face lit up as she saw the bow on Andy and then reached to hug the dog. Andy responded with a swipe of his tongue across her face, bringing out her musical laughter. She straightened up to find Teeg watching her closely.

"Triese? Do you know how beautiful you are?" Teeg reached to kiss her cheek, almost afraid to touch her. If anything was left of his heart for Triese to take, it would have been taken. "All set for a meal?"

"I am. But what about Andy? He can't come in with us." Triese was disturbed at that.

"Where we're going, he can. Did you know that we have a restaurant with an outdoor patio that allows dogs?" Teeg tucked her into his truck and then ran around to jump inside himself.

"We do? I never knew that." Triese reached to rub at Andy's ears..

"We do. And then maybe we can go for a short walk." Teeg had already checked out her shoes, seeing the lower heel on them.

"That would be nice." Triese looked out of the window, not seeing the looks that Teeg kept shooting at her.

Their meal finished, Teeg reached for Triese's hand and walked towards the river path. Andy trotted along beside him, his face turning up every so often to study his people. The two most favourite people in his life were together. That made him happy.

Teeg found his favourite bench and seated Triese. He sat beside her, an arm around her to draw her close to him.

"Teeg? We haven't talked about what happened in a while. The court cases are all finished now, aren't they?" Triese thought that they were and prayed that if there were more, they would have the strength and grace to get through them.

"They are, darling. They are. I am glad that they are done but if it hadn't been for this, I would not have met the love of my life." Teeg waited for Triese to understand his words.

Triese listened to his words, finally understanding what he was saying. She looked up at him, wonder on her face.

"Teeg? What are you saying?" Triese didn't think that she had heard him correctly.

"I love you, Triese. You are the one who brightens my day, keeps me centred and grounded, and sees the best in me. I love you. I want to spend whatever time God has for us on earth with you. Will you marry me, be the bride of my heart?" Teeg held up the ruby ring that he had found, knowing that he thought of her as a price above rubies.

Triese stared at him before she remembered to snap her mouth closed. She blinked back her tears before she nodded. Teeg slipped the ring on her finger before he reached to kiss her. They both began to laugh as Andy tried to get between them, to get in on their joy. Triese hugged him, laughter sparkling on her face. She then sat back against Teeg, hearing his prayer for their decision and life that they would plan together. She was grateful that he was a praying man.

They sat there for a long time, Andy content to lie across their knees. It would become a favourite position for him.

"I was so afraid, Teeg, that you would be killed."

"I was the same for you. And for Tait. It is hard to understand the depravity of some people."

"It is hard to understand, but it is life without God. He was our Shield and Protector in all that we face. He proved that in more ways than one over that time of trial." Triese had learned to trust God more and more over the past months.

A movement to her right had her turning her head that way. Wonder filled her face as she saw John standing there, a slight light glowing around him. Her hand tightened on Teeg's and caused him to look that way as well.

"John?" Teeg's voice was hushed as they watched the light fade and John disappear.

They shared a look with one another, neither ready to speak.

"He was an angel, Teeg. An angel sent by God just for us. I know that he's the one who rescued Tait."

"I am sure that he was. God does that, you know." Teeg hugged her close to him, content to hold his love in his arms and know that they would walk through life hand in hand. God had been their Shield and Protector over their trials and troubles.

Dear Readers:

Thank you for choosing to read the story of Teeg and his lady, Triese, and of course, his dog, Andy. I was doing my devotions about a month ago and was struck by the thought that God is our Shield and Protector. From that thought grew this novel. It is how it works with me.

Their story evolved, as do all my works, over the course of the novel. I never know where they'll take me. The idea of poaching animal organs was not what I had thought for the story, but it is what evolved given their work.

I am always happy to have other characters walk into stories. They always add to the plot and solution of the stories. Richard's team is in *His Protectors*. Brandon and Hagen, Burnie and Muir, and Buckley and Locklin are part of *The Barnabas Chronicles*. Dallas story is *Dallas: Called to Return.* They always try to help solve it and are usually successful. Heath and Hannah, the adorable toddlers, are known to the characters as ones who will smother with kisses and hugs and refuse to return to their parents.

God is our Shield and Protector. My father would often say that we had no idea what we had been protected from. I have to agree with his words. I miss his words of wisdom greatly. He was a quiet man, never said a lot, but what he said was always thought out and Bible-based. I am also convinced that God sends angels just as we need them. I had experiences as a teenager with stray dogs who walked me home and then disappeared.

Once more, thank you for coming along on this journey.

God bless each one of you.

Ronna

www.ingramcontent.com/pod-product-compliance
Lightning Source LLC
Chambersburg PA
CBHW070350200726
48294CB00003B/825

* 9 7 8 1 9 9 8 8 2 1 3 7 2 *